STILL

A second chance romance novella

By

Lizzie Stanley

Sisters by choice...

Cover design by Maldo Designs.

Holly, this one is for you.

I will never stop being thankful to you for your
tireless friendship and love, and the way you reiterate
and underline it every single day. We are family.

Hollywood + Amersham forever xoxo

I meant every word

Thank you for
your presence in
my life.

Love you loads,

Content warning:

To be able to make an informed decision as to whether this book is for you, please be advised this story contains the following:

- Underage teen pregnancy
- Childbirth
- Talk of birth related mental trauma
- Car accident
- Hospital waiting room scene
- Discussion of injury, specifically broken bones

Your mental health matters!

Chapter 1

Then

Nat and Tim are both 15

Nat

"You're *bloody lucky* I'm not pressing charges against your son!" My mother screams at Tim's enraged father and sobbing mother, before whirling on me and putting her finger in my face for the hundredth time since the doctor's appointment earlier today. "And you," she snarls, lost to her fury, "should be thankful your father isn't alive to see this. It would have *killed* him."

My eyes fill with tears at that low blow, but I just meet her gaze, refusing to break down in front of her. Not after a comment like that.

I just want to die right now.

"You are *not* calling the police about this," Mr Stewart says in a tone that brooks no opposition. Predictably, it makes Mum bristle, but he ploughs on. "Say what you want about Tim, but it takes two to tango." My skin crawls, even though I knew someone was going to fling that *two to tango* line at me. It's the sneer he gives me that finally puts my head in my hands. If I don't look, I won't see it. It's the same scant comfort a child clings onto.

Like the one I'm now carrying.

"How could this *happen*..." Mrs Stewart sounds utterly

heartbroken, and that's worse than any anger I've had thrown my way. "You're not old enough, either of you…"

I make myself look up, and my eyes don't fall on her. They go straight to Tim. My love. My boyfriend. The only person I've ever felt good around. He's white as a bed sheet, sat there all muddy after football practice, his kit damp with sweat. Just a kid, home from his sports club, the furthest thing from a father figure you can imagine. He's pulled his mop of thick brown hair in all directions, and the shattered expression on his face will live rent free in my head forever. I know it takes two. I *know* this. But I can't get over the feeling that I'm the one who just ruined his life.

Tim's the best person I know. He's smart and he's kind and he's gentle, and I'm so in love with him. And, somehow, *he* loves *me*. He *loves* me. As soon as he enters the room, I light up and feel like my insides are fizzing. Better still, he looks at me the same way, automatically reaching for my hand every time I turn up like we're two halves of the same whole finally coming back together. It's like nothing and no-one else even exists when we're together, whether that's sitting next to each other in class, or walking home hand in hand, or…

'Doing our homework' in one of our bedrooms.

It went too far. We knew it at the time. But it was like we couldn't help ourselves, like our love for each other took possession of us and overrode all common sense. He did get condoms, but the first time we used one, we didn't really know what we were doing so it might not have gone on right. *I* thought it did, though. His fingers may have been shaking as he rolled it on, but he took his time and didn't rush. He wanted to do it properly, so we didn't end up…well, in the exact position we're in now.

And there was this one time when we didn't have one, but we wanted each other so desperately that he pulled out and we just hoped for the best. The same way we were warned never to do in sex ed. But it seems the universe likes to screw kids over, while simultaneously screwing over older people who *want* a baby and can't have one no matter how hard they try. If I was twenty-five and did withdrawal, I wouldn't be in these shoes, I know it in my bones. Life is just that cruel.

But that doesn't matter, because now I'm four months pregnant before I've even hit the age of consent, and these adults don't care that Tim and I are just young and in love and made a mistake. They just see two stupid, oversexed kids who mucked up everyone's lives with their recklessness.

"Can I just - " Tim speaks up in a voice that somehow sounds so young, even though his voice has already broken, but Mr Stewart cuts across him.

"Timothy Louis Stewart, you do not say a *single* word," he spits close to Tim's ear. I've never liked Mr Stewart.

"Natalie was supposed to be attending a *Sadler's Wells program* after this academic year. Do you have *any idea* how hard we've worked to get there?!" I swear Mum is more upset about that than anything else. *I'm* more than a little heartbroken, too, not that it seems to matter to her. Dancing is my life, and I was beyond thrilled to get a place there. It was my dream since I was tiny. The first time I was taken to a dance show, I was enraptured by the performers, the way they moved and twisted so gracefully in time to the music, and in that moment I found my passion, my life's purpose. And after all the discipline and hard work, all of the parts of myself I gave to it, it was all finally within reach, only a case of marking time until I finished my GCSEs and then got the chance to learn from the best dancers in the country and become a respected professional dancer. Maybe even end up in a West End show.

It's all gone now. Placed out of my reach forever. Aside from the time out of my training regime and the time it would take to get back up to speed, I will have a child to parent. I won't be able to give as much of my time and my attention to dancing as I did before. And the West End? Forget it. I'd never be able to keep up with rehearsals and performances.

I place a hand on my abdomen, still mostly flat. This poor little one didn't mean any harm. I'm abruptly sorry for feeling sorry for myself, when his or her mere existence has been made the subject of angry arguing and mud-slinging before they even get here. It's not the baby's fault. No child deserves that. They should be loved and wanted, not regretted and resented.

Oh my god. Is this…are these the first stirrings of motherhood? Of loving and defending the baby inside me from any and all comers? I wrench my mind away from the question, scared to answer it even to myself. Scared of what I'm becoming.

"Yeah, well, what about Tim? My son had a bright future ahead of him before your daughter spread her legs - "

Tim stands and glares at his father. "You don't speak about Nat that way again," he warns his outraged father. "Not ever. Do you hear me?" My heart almost stops beating at how steady his voice is as he stands up for me. It packs more of a punch than if he'd shouted it. Gratitude floods my heart; he *does* still feel the same way I do. It *can* still be us against the world.

Before Mr Stewart can open his mouth to shout any more abuse, a red-headed whirlwind enters the room, jabbing her finger in his face the way my mother did in mine. "Now is not the time for your stinking misogyny, *father dear*," Sadie snaps. She was sent to her room when my mother banged on the Stewarts' door, barging in to break the news that I'm having Tim's baby and it's too late for an abortion. I guess Tim's twin didn't do as she was told; she's my friend, and, knowing her the way I do, I'm surprised she even agreed to leave the room. "What you just said to Nattie was disgusting, and you should apologise to her for it."

"Sadie," Mrs Stewart begins in a shaky voice, holding her hands out to placate her, but Mr Stewart has gone purple.

"Keep out of it and *go back to your room*," he seethes. I wonder if Sadie barged in to deliberately take the heat off us, distracting her dad to give Tim and me a moment to breathe. From the way their dad glares at her, she couldn't have done a better job.

While tempers fray and voices get louder and louder, Tim looks across at me. His dear boyish face, normally so full of warm smiles and good cheer, has crumpled. I've never seen him so close to tears before, not once since Mum and I moved to Foxton two years ago. I liked him straight away, but we've only been properly going out since the end of Year Ten, when he invited me to the cinema and paid for both tickets *and* a large popcorn that we shared. I don't remember which movie we saw. I only remember the way his smile made my soul gallop.

Our eyes meet, and the depth of the desperate apology I see in his bright blue eyes makes me want to weep. I can almost hear what he's thinking: *I'm so sorry I did this to you.* Like he feels responsible, and ashamed. Just like I felt. I shake my head, refusing to let him feel like the guilty party. We *both* did this. This is something we did together, not something that he did to me. Anyone who says otherwise is not just wrong, but disgusting.

"We'll do what we can to help," Mrs Stewart begins.

"Quiet," Mr Stewart barks at her at the same time Mum snipes, "Well, I should think so, too," but she brushes them both off.

"We *will*," she insists, quiet but dignified. She's always been sweet to me, and she's still looking at me with kindness, even though I've just come over and upended her entire world, and put her cantankerous husband in a foul temper.

"And what does that mean?" Mum scoffs. "Can you salvage her

place in one of the best dancing schools in the world?"

Tim's mum sighs. "I know it's awful that she can't go, but…but we will help take care of the baby. We'll make sure responsibility is taken."

"Are you sure it's Tim's baby, young lady?" Mr Stewart asks me suddenly. He's deadly serious, burning into me with a sharp, inquisitor's stare. I can almost feel the lamp burning into my eyes, and it gets worse when he takes a step towards me, looming forward like he *wants* to intimidate me. I'm shocked rigid, but maybe I shouldn't be, maybe I should have expected this question. My voice has frozen in my throat, but I'm saved from the need to answer.

"Dad!" Sadie shouts, but Tim once again stands, his fists clenching at his side.

"Say you're sorry. *Right now*." His voice is shaking with fury, even worse than before. "Say you're sorry for what you just said." I've never seen that look in his eyes; Tim is the most easygoing person you could wish to meet, a direct contrast to his fiery twin. But from the inferno blazing on his face, I think he'll strangle his dad in a rage if he doesn't take that question back in the next ten seconds.

Even Mr Stewart seems to realise he's gone too far this time. "I… I had to ask. I *did*."

"No. You didn't. Apologise to Nat, *now*." Half of me wants to run out of this house; the other half wants to rush into Tim's arms, where I know I'll feel safe forever after how he's shown up for me in this moment, against a father who unnerves him. He's confided in me several times about how his father's iron fist and filthy moods brings the whole atmosphere down in his home and make him feel like hell. For him to stand toe to toe with him for my sake in this way… It's proof, though I didn't need it, that I couldn't ask for a better person to be loved by.

Tim will never treat our child the way his dad treats him. I know that like I know grass is green.

"Her name is *Natalie*, not 'Nat' - " Mum protests.

"I'm sorry," Mr Stewart mutters, not looking at me. It's still way more than I was expecting.

"Apology accepted," I whisper back, and he gives me a filthy look, because my response agrees he had something to apologise for.

Just like Tim, I'll have to protect this baby from that man. He's not going to frighten them with his bullishness if I have anything to say about it.

"I've told my daughter, and I expect you to tell your son," my mother interjects, "that their relationship is over as of now. I refuse to allow them to spend any unsupervised time together, and I will be contacting the school to make arrangements to keep them separated."

"Of course." Mr Stewart stares his son down. "They've shown they can't be trusted, and there's a baby to consider now. Don't look at me like that," he snaps at his son, whose glare is a mix of fury and panic. "You both made choices, and now you have to live with the consequences. Your teenage romance is not more important than that child's welfare. And I'm not having you pulling this stunt again and adding even more brats to this, this... *madness*."

Stunt.

Brats.

I wish I could slap him.

Tim's eyes dart to me, and I tell him with my own that this separation is not what I want, by a long shot. We're supposed to be going to the fairground tomorrow. He's been promising me he'll win me one of those giant teddy bears, or a goldfish. We were going to go on the ferris wheel. *Fat chance now.* When Mum issued this demand on the way over here that he and I would break up, I told her no, and that she couldn't make me. I was informed I did not have a choice. But I do. Don't I?

Maybe Tim and I could run away together. I didn't have the chance to tell him what was happening before now. I only found out about being pregnant today, when I fainted after my morning shower and Mum took me to the doctor during her lunch break. I hadn't really noticed anything before that; my periods have never been regular, and I put that time I threw up a few weeks ago down to a stomach bug. I've been extremely tired lately, sure, but my dance training is rigorous, and I had no reason to think it was because of anything other than overdoing it during practice.

We can't stick around with things the way they are. So it might be for the best if we just…run off. If Tim and I could get enough money together to just jump on a train and find a place to rent wherever we end up… We could both get jobs, maybe. And we could scrape together enough to survive, just us and our baby, and not get torn apart by angry grown-ups who think they know best and have no regard for what Tim or I are thinking and feeling.

No, we couldn't, my common sense says sadly. We're too young. We'd never be able to rent anywhere or get jobs that could pay our bills. There's nowhere we can go, nobody that can help us. We'd end up on the streets. We wouldn't make it in a million years.

My heart wails at that knowledge, that we're stuck here, with these people calling the shots. It's the craziest sort of mess: we're old enough to procreate, but not old enough for autonomy and the freedom to handle this situation by ourselves.

Well, come what may, I'm not giving Tim up, I promise myself.

Not now. Not ever.

Tim

I can't feel my legs.

Or my hands.

My poor Nattie. I've ruined her life. That dance program was everything to her, and she was going to go all the way with it. Watching her on the stage when I've gone to her performances has always given me butterflies. She was genuinely born to dance. And I've taken that away from her because I just couldn't resist sliding inside of her.

I feel like I could pass out as I watch Mrs Karas pull Nat to her feet, and she doesn't do it gently. "Right, well, we're leaving now."

"Don't yank her around like that," I snap, not thinking things through, just driven by an urge to protect my...

Oh, right. We're not allowed to be girlfriend and boyfriend anymore.

Guess I'll just call her my everything, then.

"Excuse me?" Her mother sounds incredulous with outrage.

"I said *don't yank her around.* She's pregnant," I mutter.

She steps forward and glares at me with all the rage in her heart. "And who's fault is that," she hisses, almost spitting with fury. "What you did was immoral, and it was *illegal*, and my daughter's life is ruined because you couldn't keep your stupid pecker in your stupid pants. How *dare* you speak to me like that, you selfish little shit, when you've destroyed everything for her?"

Fuck. She's right.

I'm the one who put a baby inside Nat. And I can't even begin to think about what that means for her. For me. *For the kid.*

I fight not to cry, because those days need to be behind me now. I don't have the luxury of breaking down. I'm needed. Nat and the…baby…they need me to step up, to be a *father*. Because I'm not going to punk out on them. If I have to go to court and have them *make* Mrs Karas give me access, I will.

"I dare," I say, very quietly but as clear as I can, "because she's the mother of my child."

"And that's not something to brag about, *or* something to throw at me," she snaps as Dad clips me round the ear. It's not the first time he's put hands on me, but it's not a common occurrence. It does its job, though; I'm shocked into silence.

"Now, get in the car, Natalie." The look Mrs Karas gives me should be able to kill me. But it's the look on Nat's face that makes me want to die as her mother pulls her - more gently - towards the door. Nat's crying, and I can't stand it. *I won't let them tear us apart -*

My fucking father grabs both of my arms and pulls them behind me, holding me back as I try to go to her. I turn my head to shout at him to fuck off, to let me comfort the girl I love, but he says in my ear, "If you don't simmer down, I will make you regret it for the rest of your life." *I don't care.* "I'll drag her into court and make her prove that bastard child is yours." I freeze. That *motherfucker.*

Fine. But he can't stop me saying this. "I love you," I assure her, not blinking.

"I love you," she says in a broken whimper.

"Oh, shut up," my father shouts at us both.

"Please," Mrs Karas sneers at me. "You're all of fifteen years old, you stupid boy. You don't even know what love is. Neither of you."

Chapter 2

Then

Nat and Tim are both 15

Nat

There is not a single part of my life that brings me any happiness now. Not one.

I'm stuck in a body that feels nothing like my own and from which I cannot escape. Always swollen, always achy, permanently nauseated but rarely ever allowed the relief of throwing up, and so far past tired that it scares me. Food doesn't taste the same, so much of it suddenly disgusting to the point of loathsome. And the baby must be gearing up to be a dancer, like I used to be, because he or she turns somersaults more than they ever stay still. God, I wish so much that they'd stop leaning on my bladder. That'd make life a little easier.

Still, the teachers give me free reign to take as many toilet breaks as I need during lessons. That's about the only positive in my days: not wetting myself.

Every morning for the past three months, it's been the same. I get up after a lousy night's sleep. Sometimes I dry heave for a while, sometimes I don't. Either way, I get stared down by my mother at the breakfast table. She only ever speaks to me in a clipped, matter-of-fact tone, mad that I couldn't get an abortion, madder still that I even suggested adoption. I don't understand her thought processes; I just know that she's determined to be angry with me in some capacity. After swallowing that sad fact once again, I put on my new school uniform: a man's white shirt, the largest school jumper they stock, and elasticated trousers. Oh, and wider fit shoes, because my feet have spread. That was unexpected.

Once I'm at school, the garbage really begins. Everywhere I go, all I hear are whispers, laughing, and snide comments. *There she is… Jesus, she's huge…* The drama of my being a pregnant teenager never seems to lose its lustre for my classmates. I've always felt a bit like the odd one out, having only started here in Year Nine when everyone else has been in the same class since Year Seven. But now… Now I'm a spectacle. *The Pregnant Girl in 11B.* Famous school wide. They did a bloody assembly about what happened to me and the importance of not having sex at all ever until you're old and married. I'm a cautionary tale, a silly slag whose inability to rein in her horniness destroyed her promising future in dancing. Nobody cares how much I miss it, and my classes, and the feel of twisting and twirling to the rhythm of the music until I feel like we're one and the same. As far as they're concerned, it's my own stupid fault and no more than I deserve.

My friends are a mixed bag: either they've hung back, not wanting to be thought as big a slut as me, or they're like Sadie, fiercely protective and daring anyone to look at me funny. Despite how painful it is sometimes to look at Sadie's eyes, the exact same colour and shape as Tim's, I genuinely don't know what I would have done without her over the last few weeks. She makes sure I have everything I need, stares down the people who watch me like I'm an ant under a magnifying glass, and has been sent to the Head's office three times for shouting at people who say rude things to me. One of them was a teacher. She got three days of detention for that.

As if all this wasn't enough, it's GCSE year, our final exams looming in the near future. We've done our mocks already, and I flunked them spectacularly. A few months ago I'd have been devastated, but I barely even care anymore, if I'm honest. It's all too much. Why should I give a shit about my grades when I'm a few short weeks away from having to *give birth to a baby*?

Oh, that's another thing. The endless blood tests and physical exams. The doctors are watching me like a hawk because I'm so young, and every test I can be sent for, I'm given. It doesn't matter that I'm scared of needles, petrified of them in fact, and so tired of being poked and prodded. I don't matter anymore. Only the baby does. And it feels like nobody cares that I spend my days rigid with fear and revulsion over what's happening to me. And… What if I die? Will that matter, or will they just be glad they saved the baby and consider me collateral damage?

One thing's for certain: I never, ever want to do this again. Not *ever*.

And I'm not even allowed to face all this heartache with the support of the boy I love. Interestingly, and much to his obvious mortification, Tim is treated by the boys like a total legend because he can *prove* he's not a virgin. Even some of the older male teachers have been giving him wry approving looks for having sperm that clearly works. The same teachers who call him a 'young tiger' call me a 'silly little tramp'.

I hate them all. I wish they'd just let me speak to him. Hold his hand for a few seconds. Let me tell him about the way the baby had hiccups inside me the other day and how funny that felt. But we're kept as separate as chlorine and acid, too big a risk to allow to mix.

During the meeting where we broke the news of my pregnancy to the Head and our form tutor, Tim's parents and mine requested - demanded - that he and I wouldn't be allowed to interact, even if supervised. They wanted to completely kill any chance we had of any physical contact, even though the damage was already done. It didn't make any sense, but they couldn't be persuaded otherwise, no matter what promises we offered or how much we begged. So he was moved into a different form group, and our timetables were changed so we didn't share any classes anymore. We're even kept apart during our lunch breaks. I'm escorted to the drama studio; he's kept in the sports hall. I think if our parents could have made it that we didn't so much as *look* at each other, they would have.

Sadie does her best to act as a go-between, and I live for the times she recites messages he's made her memorise for me. It's something I cling to when the days get hard, as they always do. I know he still loves me. He knows I still love him. All we can do is wait and see what happens, and hope that our families will one day relax enough to just let us breathe the same air as each other.

I have another two months or so to go before the baby comes, which still doesn't seem real to me. It's doing well and is developing at the right rate, and at least there's nothing wrong there; but despite having another person literally living inside me, this is the loneliest I've ever been.

And the weekends, where I don't even see Tim - or anyone - in passing, are the worst days of all. Unfortunately, this was my last week at school before Mum pulls me out for homeschooling for the rest of my pregnancy. I've only been in school this long because the Head said this was what had happened in previous cases and Mum didn't want to piss off the school or the local education authority. Now, though, I'm too close to full term for the school to be comfortable having me there on a daily basis, in case my water breaks in the middle of geography or whatever.

So I have a heavy heart on this particular Friday lunchtime, because after today I have weeks and weeks of solitude with no respite, stuck in an atmosphere so thick with recrimination you could cut it with a knife. In the months since the doctor's appointment, Mum has never fully calmed down, and I'm now quite sure she is never going to forgive me. I've been hoping that she would eventually show me some kindness, having been through a pregnancy herself and because she can see how miserable it's making me. But her anger is stronger than her empathy for her daughter.

"It's gonna be OK," Sadie whispers to me as we pack up after maths. Lunch is about to start, and I can already see Mrs Singh getting ready to escort me to my designated lunch room. I sigh heavily. "No, really," she insists, staying quiet and sliding me her textbook and pointing to a note she pencilled in next to the printed algebra sums.

When we get to the courtyard, I'm going to create a diversion. Go to the boy's loos next to the music room. TRUST ME.

I stifle a gasp, and we exchange a meaningful look. I know she's been trying to get Tim and me some time together, but the teachers have been relentlessly conscientious in their mission to prevent that.

"Ready to go, Natalie?" Mrs Singh gives me a gentle smile. She's been one of the more pleasant staff members to deal with; no judgemental looks or arch jokes to build her street cred with the other pupils. Small mercies.

Sadie links arms with me. "As we'll ever be," she chirps. I'm allowed to have some company at lunchtime, thank god.

My heart is beating at a mile a minute as we head down the stairs and through the double doors. *Will I really get to see him?* Even the possibility has lit me up like a Christmas tree. The baby is wriggling around inside me like a kitten on catnip, probably wondering why I'm so fired up. Every cell in my body is on high alert. I only know the scantest details of this plan, but I know I'm going to have to move quickly, and that is no mean feat right now, the state I'm in.

With a final squeeze of my elbow, Sadie suddenly kicks off. "ALEX!" she shouts at the very top of her lungs to a friend of ours, who's waiting close to the door. It makes me jump, and I knew to expect it. Mrs Singh lets out a startled squeak. "I want a fucking word with you!"

"Oh yeah?" Alex starts storming over, clearly primed for the task. "What's your problem?"

Sadie squares up, jabbing her finger in Alex's face. "Where the *fuck* do you get off, switching to Team Jacob, *and then* annotating the copy of *Eclipse* I loaned you?! It was *signed by Jackson Rathbone*!"

"That's enough!" Mrs Singh starts, but Alex pipes up.

"It was *not*, you *lied* about that, you ginger *wench*!" And, because they're seemingly going for broke, they start shoving each other, making the fight physical as well as verbal. It's so believable that, if I didn't know them better, I'd be worried. Instead, I want to applaud their performance.

Sadie waves me away behind her back, and it galvanises me into action. As quickly and as quietly as I can, I head towards the music room, keeping my head down as I pass a couple of boys in their football cleats, the type who normally treat me to off-colour remarks. I'm deaf to them in this moment, tingling all over when I shove the door to the boys' toilets open, ignoring the weird sweat-and-watch-straps smell and the dingy blue walls.

Because he's there.

As soon as Tim dashes over to me and pulls me into his arms, I start to cry. My emotions are all over the place at the best of times - thanks, hormones - but right now, finally being held by Tim again, even in such an unromantic setting, and enjoying the scent of his skin and hearing him tell me he's got me... It's all too much. And nowhere near enough.

He hustles us into one of the cubicles in case anyone else comes in, and I carry on falling apart in his arms the way I've wanted to for weeks now.

"Are you OK?" he asks me, kissing my hair and cupping my jaw with gentle hands. "I've missed you so much, are you OK?" He presses our foreheads together, and for long moments we just breathe each other in. I can feel his hands trembling, and it's both heartbreaking and blissfully reassuring to know I'm not the only one miserable at our separation.

If anyone walks in, I'll keel over and die at the unfairness of it. All I've wanted in the past three months is finally here, and I don't know how I'm ever going to let go of him at the end of these few stolen minutes. Because this *isn't* wrong. The way we feel about each other isn't dirty or juvenile or something to be sorry for. And nor is our baby, who is at least born of love, even if they will be here sooner than is ideal.

Realising that he hasn't yet felt our baby move, I take Tim's hand and put it on my stomach, sending a silent plea to our son or daughter to move for Daddy right now. I want him to feel this. He's missed out on so much, thanks to our angry and narrow minded families, and they're not things he can get back another time.

Thankfully, the little one obliges, fistbumping their father hard through my belly. And his face…the wonder on it, the amazement in his beautiful blue eyes, will stay with me and sustain me for a long time. "Oh my god," he whispers, and bends in the cramped cubicle to kiss my stomach, making my eyes fill up again. "Hey," he says quietly to the baby, "it's…all gonna be fine. I'll *make* it fine. I…I promise."

Just when I think I couldn't be more in love with him…

When he straightens back up, his face becomes determined. "Listen. Jacob said he'd help us." I blink in surprise. Jacob is Tim's older brother, and always seemed so remote and timid. I've barely spoken to him, other than a quick hello every now and again, and he always stayed out of the way as much as possible, staying in his room more often than not. "He said he'd take notes from me and leave them for you somewhere you'll find them on his evening bike rides. Can you tell me somewhere? Under a plant pot, maybe?"

I think. "On the wall by the gate... The little lion statue is loose. He can put them under there, if he's careful."

"Right." Tim looks as thrilled as I am about this prospect of communicating with each other again. Our mobile phones have been confiscated, and I don't have access to my email account anymore. My mum and his parents must be hurting so much to be so ruthlessly cruel. But we've found a way.

We will always find a way back to each other. I know that now.

So, even when Mr Ratcliffe finds us, and even when Tim is sent to the Head's office with Sadie and Alex for punishment, I keep smiling to myself, feeling calmer than I have in longer than I'd care to remember. We'll win.

In the end, Tim and I will win, no matter what they try to do.

Chapter 3

Now

Nat and Tim are both 30

Tim

My phone rings just as I'm heading into my two o'clock meeting. I frown when I see it's my daughter. *Something's wrong.* She never calls me at work.

Nodding at my boss through the glass wall of the conference room, I pick up. "Hey, El."

"Dad?!" Her voice is cracking, high with panic.

"What's the matter? What's going on?" Everything else vanishes around me. I can't remember the last time I heard Eleanor sound like this.

"Dad…" She begins crying as she talks, gasping between sobs and syllables. My stomach plummets as she continues. "We were in a crash. Me a-and Mum. We're at the h-hospital…"

I don't even tell my boss I'm not going to be able to attend the meeting that's now starting. I just start speed walking back to my desk to pick up my keys. "Eleanor, are you OK?" *Please, let my baby girl be unhurt.* She's talking on the phone. That's got to be a good sign, right? She's only fifteen. She should be *exempt* from harm.

"I'm fine. It's… Oh, god… Mum's hurt…"

Fuck. "OK, sweetheart, I'm on my way. Are you at Foxton General, or St Mary Magdalene's?"

"Foxton General. They're taking her to surgery…" *Jesus.* My heart twists the way it does every time my little girl cries. This time, though it physically hurts. Because this isn't a scraped knee or a lost toy, something easily rectified, like when she was small. This is real life being vicious and frightening. And my gut feels hollow at the thought of Nat being so badly injured that she needs to get operated on.

"Alright. Where are you? Are there people around?"

"Yes. There are, like, tons of nurses, so I'll be fine. I'm sitting in the waiting room at A and E."

"OK. *Stay right there.* Don't go anywhere, and stay close to those nurses. I'll be there as fast as I can." There's no time to waste waiting for the lift, so I run hell for leather down ten flights of stairs to the staff car park.

Images of Nat go screaming through my head. From when we were teenagers walking home together, and when we threw Eleanor's fifth birthday party and she helped our daughter blow out the candles on the cake I made, to the last time I saw her a couple of days ago on her way out to teach her dancing class. Her hair was piled high in a clip, and her leotard…the way it clung… *I tried so hard not to notice.* The way she pronounces all her Ts and Hs, never skipping them, thanks to her strict mother. She's been a constant throughout the years as we learned together and grew together as parents. She's everything to me, just like El. *Please, god, not Nat. I couldn't take it if she's…*

I force myself to pay attention to my driving on the way to the hospital, the same one where Eleanor was born fifteen years ago. The last thing she or anyone else needs is for me to get into a car wreck as well. *She's OK. They* both *are. It's all gonna be fine.* Maybe if I wish for this insistently enough, it'll have an impact on reality.

Someone in the sky is on my side because I find a parking space straight away, which is fortunate because I'd have just stopped anywhere and settled the parking fine later. I race through the automatic doors and damn near skid to a stop by the front desk, where a nurse is tidying up some paperwork. "Natalie Karas? She was brought in after a car crash."

The nurse on duty spends what feels like ages looking it up on her computer. "How are we spelling Karas today?" I tell her, gritting my teeth because I will never be one of those people who shout at hospital staff. "Are you family?"

I pause, not knowing how to begin to answer that question. *Not technically, but in practice, absofuckinglutely.* Fortunately, Eleanor picks that moment to appear and throw her arms around me. "Daddy," she sobs, and my arms automatically go around her, my knees shaking with relief that she's here and upright and doesn't appear bloodied or swathed in bandages.

"El." It comes out as a huge exhale of breath. "Are you OK?"

She nods, then shakes her head against me and cries harder.

The nurse clears her throat gently. "Miss Karas is being operated on right now. I'll take you to the waiting area."

When we get there, Eleanor sniffs as the nurse leaves. "She looked at you like you were a snack," she sneers, never a fan of women noticing her Pops.

I ignore the comment. "You're OK? Pinky promise?"

She nods dully. "Yeah. Just a few knocks and bruises. And I want to punch the driver who rear ended us, right in his tiny little testicles. But otherwise...yeah, I got lucky." Sometimes Eleanor sounds just like Sadie, and I'd smile if I wasn't feeling so sick about what's taken place. *I could have lost my daughter.*

I could still lose Nat.

Not that she's even mine to lose, but tell that to my aching heart.

"What happened?" I sit us both down in the blue plastic seats screwed to the wall. They're uncomfortable, but it doesn't matter. Nothing matters until I know what we're looking at here, and if the mother of my child is OK or not.

She wipes her eyes. "It was horrible... He hit us really hard from behind, and we spun around, and kept on spinning." More tears fall, and her chin wobbles. Just like when she was a toddler, crying as I dropped her off because she wanted to be with both Mummy *and* Daddy.

"It's OK, I've got you," I murmur, giving her hand a little squeeze.

"And M-Mum was trying to steer, but...and then..." Her shoulders judder as she loses control again. "There was this wall...it was heading right for me...and Mum..." She hiccups. "Mum threw the steering wheel around, and she made it so that *she* hit the wall instead of me. She saved my life, and now she... She's in..." And with that, she leans forward, bent double, sobbing her eyes out.

My own are damp as a riot of emotions smash through me. Rage at the driver who hit them, who would do well to never cross my path. Sympathy for my daughter, who must be feeling awful right now, even though none of this is her fault. And, above all, desperate gratitude to Nat for doing whatever she had to do to protect Eleanor and taking the brunt of the damage in her place. I will *never* be able to repay her for that.

Assuming I even get the chance. "What's the damage for your mum? Has anyone said?"

She pushes her hair back with both hands. "They said she's broken her legs, and that she'll need surgery to fix them. That's where she is now."

"Was she conscious?"

"Yes. Told me not to worry about her, but I could tell…sh-she was in pain." She leans her head in the crook of my shoulder, and I pull her close. "Oh my god, what if she can't dance anymore, Dad? It'd be all my fault…if she hadn't swerved - "

"Hey." I give her a gentle shake. "Don't you ever think like that. If I'd been the one driving, I'd have done the exact same thing. Your mum and I love you more than anything in the world, and we would do *anything*, not limited to sacrificing our lives, to keep you safe and unharmed. And neither one of us would hesitate or regret it. OK?"

I know it doesn't exactly make her feel *better*, but she at least understands now that this is a choice her mother would have made a million times over, because the alternative is not just unthinkable to us, but unbearable to even contemplate.

And, as we wait, my arms around her so she feels more secure, I can only hope that the *other* alternative - where Nat is never OK again - is not the trade-off for my daughter's life. I know Eleanor, and that will cast a dark shadow over the rest of her days.

To say nothing of the shadow it would cast over my own.

I still love you.

These are the words that spring to my mind first when I see Nat lying in her hospital bed, still groggy from the anaesthesia, her neck wrapped in a foam brace. Typical Nat, she's muttering soothing words to Eleanor and stroking her hair as she holds her, comforting her daughter when *she's* the one banged up in a hospital bed.

I don't think *how are you feeling.*

Or *can I get you anything or do anything at all for you.*

Not even *thank you for saving our daughter at the expense of your own wellbeing.*

Just those four little words that I've been smothering inside myself for the past fifteen odd years, ever since she and I decided to just focus on our little girl and put our relationship to one side. Being a couple just seemed like such a gamble, when we were so young and shell shocked and exhausted by parenthood, and when we were still children ourselves. We wanted Eleanor to have the stability she deserved from her family, as well as all of our focus, not sparing any for loving each other. As if we'd even have had the energy, anyway. Now the idea just seems shockingly stupid and a waste of precious time. Yes, we were so very young, and confused, but we were also desperately in love.

And I, for one, still am. I always will be; there's no escaping it, and I'd never want to, no matter what.

I need to face up to that, instead of ignoring it like a dickhead and pretending it's all in the past. Even if she's no longer in this with me, which she might not be. Maybe she's moved on the way I never could. It won't make any difference to my heart if she has; I'll still be hers and nobody else's.

Nat's smile when she sees me over El's shoulder is tired, but warm, like she's glad I'm here. Looking at her is like a punch in the gut. There's a drip in her hand, and small cuts dotted over her arms and face from being showered in broken glass from the smashed windshield. She's looking sallow with exhaustion, with dark circles around her eyes. Her hair, usually a neat, smooth brown mane that reaches her shoulders, is a total mess. It sticks up on one side and is slightly matted and tangled from the remains of blood and sweat.

She has never looked more beautiful in her life.

Before I get the chance to say anything, the blue curtains around her bed are pulled open, and then closed again by the nurse who enters the bedside area. "Hi, is this your family?" She's short and smiley, and exactly the sort of cheerful person you'd find most reassuring if you woke up in hospital.

"Yes," Nat says simply, and something inside me begins to relax at her confirmation. *We* are *family*. If nothing else, we have that undeniable fact.

"Is my mum OK? What's the bottom line? Will her legs be alright?" Eleanor fires off questions like a Gattling gun.

"El," I murmur, "slow down and let the nurse speak." My eyes meet Nat's, and her sleepy smile is everything to me in this moment. It means she's still here and not beyond reach, like she might have been.

The nurse grins. "So, in order: one, she will be," she begins, marking off the points on her fingers, "two, she has a concussion and a nasty case of whiplash. She sustained a compound fracture in her right femur, but we've managed to realign the bones and hold them in place with screws. In her left leg, she has a compression fracture in her femur and a closed fracture in her fibula, and she's going to need a brace and physical therapy. And three, yes, but there's a long road ahead in terms of recovery." She turns to me. "I'm afraid you'll have to wait on your partner hand and foot for the foreseeable future while we get her walking again."

"We aren't - " Nat begins in a strained and husky voice, but I interrupt her.

"I will," I say firmly. Because this would be *perfect*. Nat's house is fine and everything, but mine is larger and better suited to installing adjustments while she recovers. I'd get to look after her the way she needs. Besides, my bedroom, which she will be taking over, has an ensuite; hers does not.

The very least I can do is relocate to the spare room.

For a little while, at least, before I win her back. Then... I smother a dark smile. If I *am* lucky enough to finally get what I've always wanted...then you'd best believe we'll be making up for lost time the moment she's fighting fit again.

After all, it's not like I didn't warn her years ago that our time would come, in the end...

...and that she'd better be ready for it, for *me*, when it did.

Chapter 4

Now

Nat and Tim are both 30

Tim

"Man, you really are covering all bases," my brother-in-law says as he unpacks the grab rail for the shower. When Sadie married Leo, I didn't so much lose a sister as gain a brother, and one who is always ready to pitch in at a moment's notice. And thank god for it; everything I need to do to prepare for Nat's discharging would be tough to finish by myself.

"Some of it is overkill." Sadie gives me a pointed look, but she's smiling. She knows how I feel about Nat; she's always known, even when I played it down, even when I refused to talk to her about it. Twins can't fool each other, at least in our experience.

That's also how I know something is different about her. I may not be able to pinpoint exactly *what*, but she's not her usual self. Looks like she slept badly, from how heavy her eyelids look, and she keeps sipping water from her bottle.

"Like what?" I fake incredulity, but she does have a point.

She's sitting on my bed, freshly made with a brand new bed set covered in snowdrops print, Nat's favourite flower. Nat also likes scented candles, so there's a large new one on the bedside table that smells like lemon meringue pie, her favourite dessert. I've already installed a new TV on a new unit at the end of the bed. Leo's helping me install hand rails and move furniture around so she'll will be able to move around easier, and when Sadie swipes my phone from my hands, she hoots with laughter when she sees what I've been looking up. "You do *not* need an intercom system!"

Leo looks up and grins knowingly. "I can see the benefit. Have you ordered it?"

I sigh. "I was thinking about it."

"What would be the point? You're going to be checking on her constantly anyway." Sadie shakes her head at me, eyes dancing with amusement.

"Yeah, but…what if she needs me when I'm in a different room?" I shrug. "I don't want her to have to wait for anything."

"I hear that," Leo pipes up, looking thoughtful. "Maybe *we* should - "

"Forget it," Sadie cuts in.

"Hear me out," he says, crooking his finger at her. When Sadie finally wanders over after a brief stare-off, he hooks a finger in her vest strap to bring her closer. "Imagine the possibilities," he murmurs, and in and among the things he whispers to her, I hear the words '…order you to strip from another room…'

"Yeah, nope. I don't need to know this shit." I hold my hands up and glare at them both, unable to still the twitch of my lips. "You guys are gross."

"And set to get even more gross." Leo looks up at Sadie and lifts his scarred eyebrow, silently asking her a question.

Sadie rolls her eyes. "OK, OK…" She turns to me, standing up and stretching a little. "Well, it was deliberate this time…"

I frown, not getting it, until she pulls her loose smock top a little tighter to her stomach, and I see the unmistakable curve of an early baby bump. "No way!" I feel myself beaming, walking over to hug her. "Congratulations."

"Yep, he shoots, he scores. Leo knocked me up again." I snicker when he blows on a finger gun, and hug him, too.

"How does Rhiannon feel about it?" My little niece is four, so old enough to understand a little of what this means.

"Um…" They look at each other and make awkward faces. "Jury's out. One moment she's listening to my tummy and giving it kisses, the next minute she's hiding some of her toys in case the babies try to take them away from her."

"She'll get on board," Leo says confidently.

"Hold up," I say as my twin's words hit me. "You said 'babies'."

"I did, didn't I." Sadie jokingly puts her head in her hands. "Guess the Stewart family genes won a point this time. Twin boys. Found out at the scan yesterday."

"Holy shit, sis." I laugh. "Holy fucking shit."

"Two little mini-Leos on my hands in just under six months…" She shakes her head. "Help meeeeeee…"

"They could just as easily have been two little Sadies…and we already know what *one* little Sadie running around is like." From the glow of adoration in Leo's eyes, he loves everything about that scenario. "Now, sit down, woman. No heavy lifting, no tiring yourself out, or thou shalt be spanketh'd." She rolls her eyes, but acquiesces pretty readily. She's not one to sit around when there's work to be done, so I guess a twin pregnancy is already taking it out of her.

For a few moments, Leo and I team up, holding the handrail in place so we can drill it into the wall. And then, as soon as it's switched off, Sadie speaks up.

"So, since I'm relegated to the sidelines, I guess I'll just go ahead and ask." She gives me a pointed look. "Is this finally, you know, *it* for you and Nat?"

Damnit.

And she knows that all she has to do is let the silence run on, for as long as it takes, until I can't stick it anymore. I always cave.

"I don't know," I mumble, "but I hope so."

"At. Fucking. *Last*," she shouts, punching the air. "What has *taken* you so long?"

I give her a direct look. "You already know what."

"Um...*I* don't," Leo says behind me as he leans against the door. "Sadie's kept all your secrets, and I've often wondered what's kept you two apart all this time." He shrugs. "None of my business, but since it sounds like you want it to change... Happy to lend a hand, or some advice, if I can, brother." He playfully scowls at my sister. "It's not like I haven't been there." She flips him off, using her middle finger to blow him a kiss.

I consider the offer. Since I share everything with my twin anyway, and I know I can trust Leo as well, I might as well take this opportunity to get a few things off my chest. "It started out - or, rather, ended - when El was born. Nat thought we'd be better off, and more stable, if we put a pin in being a couple and focused on the baby. And I didn't like it, but I agreed that El needed to come first." I shrug. "You know how enormous it is to become a parent. Now imagine that happening in your mid teens."

"Big yikes." Leo grimaces in sympathy; Rhiannon is a feisty little handful for two full grown adults, so he has new insight into just how rough it was for us. Worth it, though.

"But...I don't know. Eleanor's getting older now, and she'll be flying the nest in just a handful of short years. And... Well, once she's standing on her own two feet, not relying on us in the same way..." I scratch the back of my neck. "I don't know. I know what *I* want, but... *So* much time has passed. Though there have been...moments." I sigh, remembering the best one, when I called into her dance studio and gave her something to think about. But that was over a decade ago. "I don't think it's ever really died. At least, it hasn't for me."

"Quick question," Leo says, looking at the ground thoughtfully, "have either of you been in a relationship since then?"

I swallow. "No. She went on a couple of dates once or twice, which damn near killed me, but nothing came of them. And the one time I tried to...*be* with anyone else...well," I feel my shoulders hunching with embarrassment. "I mean...to be crude for a second here, I was inside one woman and thinking of another, and that felt terrible, so..."

"Hmm," Sadie says, giving Leo a pointed look. "What an *interesting* way to handle not being with the woman you want."

He just swipes dust off his shoulder a la elder Luke Skywalker. "Don't act like you didn't benefit from my sluttishness while I waited for you." He narrows his eyes. "Or do I need to remind you of the series of events which landed you with a double act in your gorgeous belly, Pumpkin?" Sadie blushes, but her grin is irrepressible.

"That's enough, you two." I shake my head. "You're worse than Gomez and Morticia."

"Goals!" Leo crows.

"I accept that as the compliment it is," Sadie retorts, while her Gomez kisses up her arm and calls her *cara mia*.

"So you really haven't...you know, dated around in the intervening years?" He holds his hands up. "No judgement, I just kind of assumed you had."

"Nah." A sharp sense of longing settles on me like misty rain. "It was Nat or nobody. Like I said, I tried with someone on my course one time, and it felt like...betrayal. Like fucking someone else was - "

"Um. Eww." Oh, *great*. El's in the doorway, holding Rhiannon's hand. Rhi hero worships El like El used to with Sadie, so it's no surprise when she echoes El's sentiment with an adorable and enthusiastic, "Ewwwwwwwwwww."

I rub my eyes. "Didn't know you were there, Princess."

"Obviously." Her lip curls, and she fakes retching.

"Don't listen at doors and you won't hear things you don't want to know about your dad. That's all I'm saying."

"I was not *listening at the door*," she informs me loftily, "I was just gonna ask Aunt Sadie if RhiRhi can have an ice pop. But go off, I guess."

Leo snorts, and Sadie bites down hard on her lip before disguising her mirth by chugging some more water. "Sure she can," she says when she has better control. She peers a little closer at her daughter. "Is that eyeliner?"

"Uh-huh," Rhiannon smiles, posing with her hands under her chin like a make-up artist on TikTok. "And lisp-stick. El put it on me with a little bwush." I look over and smirk. Rhiannon's pale red hair has been put up in an elaborate ponytail with braids, and her eyes are lined in black to match her black lipstick.

"Goth princess," Leo says, scooping her up for a cuddle. "Gimme a kiss right here." He points to his cheek, and Rhi plants a smacker, leaving a thick black lip print. Leo howls like a cartoon wolf in appreciation, and she giggles. It takes me back to when Eleanor was that age, and all the hours Nat and I spent making her laugh with songs and dances and silly games that she probably won't remember now. But I always will.

Speaking of Eleanor, she gives me a look like a laser, cutting into me to see everything Nat and I have kept away from her line of vision throughout her life. She is *pissed*, and I don't quite understand why.

"Daddy, let me down," Rhi grumbles, "Mummy said yes to ice pop." She smacks the P with her smudged black lips. When Leo sets her down, she looks up at her heroine and tugs on her top. "El, Mummy said yes."

After a beat, Eleanor looks down at her mini-me and plasters on a big smile. "She did," she agrees in a bright voice, picking her up, "and now you need to decide what flavour. You can have orange, or you can have lemon, or you can have…" She continues to list each type, one by one, counting them on the fingers on one hand. El wants to work with children, and she's always very conscious of how she communicates with her cousin. It's something I really love to watch; she'd make a great teacher.

"Talk to her later," Sadie advises me wisely. "She may need to be walked through everything. Just. You know. Don't mention screwing people who aren't her mother."

I've never liked it when my daughter is subdued. It sets my parental Spidey Sense to tingling. *What's up? What does she need? How can I help her?* Eleanor has never been shy about expressing herself, just like her aunt, but when she shuts down and says nothing…that's when I know it's serious.

So when we're making dinner together, and she's talking in monosyllables whenever I ask her anything, I wait until the lasagne is in the oven before speaking. "OK, let's talk." I pull a chair out for her at the small breakfast nook and then stand opposite. She doesn't look at me as she sits. *Shit, she's really mad.* "Go for it."

She rolls her thumbs over each other, again and again, and then sighs. "Did you and Mum really stay apart because of me?"

Oh.

"Not *because* of you," I reply, "*for* you."

She rolls her eyes. "Splitting hairs much? I mean, if I'm really and seriously the only reason you two aren't together, I want you to tell me."

I think for a moment. "We wanted to make sure you had a stable and reliable family unit," I finally settle on. "We were…god, we were *your age* when you were born." I grimace as the full weight of that thought hits me. Looking at El now, there's no way she should be a parent. She's got so much she needs to do, to have the *freedom* to do.

I don't regret having her for a second. She's the black hair dyed, eyeliner loving light of my world. But seeing her at the age I was when she arrived, it's definitely made me think about things in a different way.

"Anyway," I continue, shaking it off, "we were so young, and teenage love does not have the best track record for success. And it was more important to us that you had two parents who had a good co-parenting relationship than two parents in a romantic relationship. It…seemed too big of a risk."

She considers this, nodding slowly as she does. I do the same thing when I'm thinking. "I think that's a load of old shite."

My eyebrows hit my hairline. "Pardon?"

I'm not talking about the minor curse word, and she knows it. "That sucks. It's… Yeah, I have friends whose parents divorced and hate each other, and our situation is way better than that. I can't take that away from you both. But…" She takes a shaky breath, swallowing down tears. I move to hug her, and for the first time ever, she holds a hand up to keep me away. And that, more than anything, brings home how much this has hurt her. "I've spent my whole life with basically the same thing as having divorced parents, and split my time between you both. But it might have been all for nothing."

"What do you mean?" I ask her quietly, though I suspect I know what she's going to say. It'll be the same words that have kept me awake into the early hours of the morning for years now.

She huffs, and it almost turns into a growl. "You and Mum just… randomly decided you'd probably have broken up. Why? Cos, I mean, you had no way of knowing if that would have even happened. You might have stayed together and been happy, and… Jesus, Dad, I might have *siblings* by now." She goes red, and quickly hides her face, resting her head on the work surface and muttering to herself.

Oh, shit, Princess, I know.

"It was what your mother thought was best at the time, and I said OK," I mutter. "I'm not blaming her, or passing the buck. I'm just saying it was what she wanted, and I… I was young, and scared, and I just wanted to do whatever would make her happy. Whatever that looked like. Even if it made me…" *Miserable.*

She looks up, and I can see her eye make-up has smudged a little, traces of wetness at the corners. "But it's not what you want now, right?"

I shake my head, unable to find the words but unwilling to conceal anything else from her.

"So go get her." My daughter looks at me like I'm failing maths a five year old could do. "Tell her how you feel. Do it now. We can turn the oven off and go to the hospital, and - "

"No." I grin wryly. "One, there are way more romantic settings than hospitals - "

"Erm, I beg your finest pardon? *ER, Grey's Anatomy?*"

"And two… You know your mother. She may need a little persuading. If she even feels the same way, which you and I will have to accept if that's not the case," I finish firmly.

"She does. She has to." Eleanor dismisses my concern like it's dust in the breeze. "But you're right, you may have to tread softly," she admits, grumbling.

I chuckle, and give her a considering look. "Are we OK now?"

She pulls a face. "Yes, as long as you guys stop using me as an excuse not to be together."

I shake my head and hug her. "Deal."

"And you let me brainstorm ways to get Mum back."

"…Maybe."

"Good, cos I have an idea…"

Chapter 5

Then

Nat is 16, Tim is 15

Nat

"Call him," I plead with my mother as the latest contraction dies down.

"No." Although she's holding my hand and gently wiping my forehead with a cool cloth, she remains implacable and steadfastly unwilling to let me have what I really need.

"Please," I whine weakly, leaning my head back against the rough hospital pillow. I've been at this for sixteen hours. I've already puked on a nurse's scrubs. She was pretty decent about it, but I'm still sweating and breathless and I can't believe how much pain I'm in. Mum won't let me have an epidural. She claims it's because she's concerned about potential negative effects, like all those horror stories you hear about women who can't walk for a while afterwards, or it numbs everything from the waist up and nothing from the waist down. But I can't help wondering if a part of her wants me to experience the full pain of childbirth, to teach me a lesson and make me realise the full consequences of my actions.

"You've got *me*," she says, her expression even but her voice brittle. "You don't need him here. This is enough of a circus as it is."

"He has the right to be here for - " But before I can complete that sentence, another contraction steals my breath. I can't bear this much longer. The pain is like nothing I could ever have imagined, and I envisioned plenty over the past few months. It's hot, ripping, murderous. Honestly, I wouldn't mind being dead if that's what it takes for this to stop.

This one goes on and on, and I become vaguely aware of the midwife doing yet another internal. "Yep, ten centimetres. You're ready to go," she says, her voice reassuringly steady and confident. She's been really brilliant, and my main measure of that is that she hasn't once given me side-eye for my age. It's as though, for the first time, it doesn't matter that I'm sixteen; I'm just another pregnant human on her list whose baby she needs to deliver safely.

And then the full meaning of what she says hits me, and despite everything, I squeeze Mum's hand, desperate for reassurance. I nearly cry with relief when she squeezes back and smooths my hair away from my damp face, giving me an encouraging look. If she hadn't…I'm not sure I could do this.

From then on, everything is a haze of pushing and bleeding and just plain *hurting*. People give me loud instructions and encouragement, and I'd tell them all to shut the hell up if I could catch my breath long enough. I pant through the pain as best I can, but I'm terrified out of my mind and it's beyond me. I'm not pushing right, and in the end, one of the nurses gets me to pull a towel with her in a weird tug of war. It's strange, but it works. It corrects what I'm doing, and I start making something approaching progress.

Please, just let me die, I can't do this anymore.

The hideous stretching down below is not something I ever want to experience again, and I scream just once when it feels like I'm being ripped in two. And then they finish the job with a scalpel, while I try to pretend it's not happening. The thing they use to cut me down below is so sharp and the sore tautness so intense that I barely feel anything beyond a scratch, but the idea of what they just did has me chucking up again, mercifully into a cardboard bowl thrust under my chin by a helpful nurse. I want to go home. I need this to stop, *now*. How is this happening... How is this *ever* going to work...

And then, suddenly, impossibly, yet very simply, the baby is out.

Here.

In my arms, yowling and covered in blood and white goo, and wriggling.

"It's a girl," I hear someone say, and all I can think is, *don't ever get pregnant, sweetheart.* I don't want her to suffer like this, not ever.

Some sort of instinct takes over, and I rub her back to soothe her as she cries at the outrage of leaving a warm, safe place, and being forced into this world with all its anger and loneliness and Mr Stewarts.

"I'm sorry," I whisper to her helplessly regretting inflicting this life on her. Poor little mite didn't ask for any of this: her clueless teenage mother, her resentful grandparents, her father being kept from her. I've got to shield her from as much of this heartache as possible, and I break down, weeping onto her little face, as the knowledge that I have no idea how to do that slams full force into my bewildered and frightened brain.

I hear a loud, choked sob next to me, and my mother buries her face in the pillow next to me, cupping the baby's head and stroking it blindly with one hand. I've never known my mother to cry like this. She was angry when my father died. She was angry when I got knocked up. She doesn't cry when she's upset. She shouts.

"I'm so sorry," she whimpers brokenly, and her face is red and tear streaked when she looks up at me. "Oh, Natalie, I'm so very sorry..." She looks at my baby with wonder, as though she'd been so wrapped up in her annoyance that she hadn't anticipated an actual baby arriving at the end of all this. A sweet, living, breathing newborn. Her granddaughter. "I haven't been there for you through all of this. I was just so…" She wipes her eyes and gives me a pleading, desperate smile. "Please forgive me. I promise, I'll look after you both. I'll help you. Whatever you need." She kisses my daughter's head, not caring about the goop. "Whatever *she* needs."

I'm too shattered to do anything but nod. But the blissful relief for her support that floods through me almost distracts me from the stitches currently sewing my ripped up vagina back together.

Almost.

Mum did call Tim's folks after that. Too late, but I suppose better late than never. She even asked to speak to Tim directly, so he'd know first. I appreciated that.

To hear Mum tell it, he couldn't get off the phone to leave for the hospital fast enough. The moment she got the words, "Natalie had a baby girl," out of her mouth, he didn't even let a second pass by before telling her he was on his way.

It's been around two hours since our daughter was born. Two months since Tim and I saw each other. Sixty notes left under the stone lion, retrieved by me when Mum was at work or in the shower or not looking. Every single one of them ended with the Walt Whitman quote: *Loved you then, love you still, always have, always will.* Every single one swore that he's waiting for me, that we will get through this, that everything's going to be OK.

And it is.

But not in the way he thinks.

Giving birth did something in my brain that being pregnant did not. Looking at her, being able to hold her in the flesh, sealed the deal.

My life is not my own anymore. I don't belong to me. I belong to her. She needs me, needs *us*, more than Tim and I need each other.

This little girl has been born to parents who are too young and not ready. She deserves better than that. And I love her. Just like that, whether it's a hormonal response or something deeper, I do. Enough to make sure she has everything she needs, as best as I can give it.

And I know Tim will feel the same.

When he arrives, he ignores my mother by my bed and focuses solely on me, grabbing my hand and linking our fingers together. I'm sure I still look awful, exhausted and grey, nothing like how I wanted to look the next time he saw me. But he stares at me like I'm infinitely adorable, and it puts me at ease in a way I haven't been since the last time he touched me. His mop of thick brown hair is a total mess, the shadows under his eyes purple as bruises, and his skin pale like it gets when he hasn't slept well.

"Are you OK?" he asks, kissing my fingers, "Are you OK?" I think he's clinging onto my hand to ground himself, because his grip is tight and almost shivering. He's giving me such immovable direct eye contact, as though no-one else exists or matters to him…as though I'm all that's keeping him upright.

I don't think enough people have considered the impact this whole situation has had on *Tim*. Sure, I'm the one who needed the scans and the endless blood tests and the classes and the dietary needs and all the rest of it, but he's suffered, too. And, while I've felt swamped and overloaded by people checking on me…none of these people were checking on him. They either called him a stud or treated him like a screw-up.

"I'm OK," I reassure him.

"Tim," my mother says quietly. He turns his jaw ever so slightly in her direction, still keeping his eyes on me. "I'm sorry." Mum's hugging herself, a clear tell that she's feeling bad. She did that when she told me Dad was dead, and when she lost her last but one job due to budget cuts. "I should have called you so you could be here. That was wrong of me. I apologise."

His jaw tenses, and I see him turning her words over in his mind. It's not something she can ever make right or take back. He missed the birth of his daughter because she thought she knew better. But apologising to him and admitting it was a mistake is at least a start. His silent nod of acknowledgement is something I expected he'd do; he wouldn't waste time shouting at her for something that can never be changed, and which she already sincerely regrets anyway.

Mrs Stewart walks in then, having finally caught up with her son. "Oh, I... Oh." She offers me and my mother a timid smile. "How are you, sweetheart?" she asks me. She's much easier to be around when her husband isn't there.

"Er...not too bad," I reply. I mean, I did just force an entire human out of me, and everything hurts like the fires of hell, and I've never been so utterly wiped both physically and emotionally in all my life, but for all that, I'm managing well, now that the nasty birth part is over.

It's almost a relief when a nurse wheels in the glass cot thing with our baby inside. If nothing else, my little one is a subject change and attention thief. Mrs Stewart's sharp intake of breath is audible, and, just like my mother, she melts when she looks inside. Our girl is sleeping peacefully, and I know I'm her mother - holy shit, I'm her *mother* - but she's objectively adorable. She has the tiniest fingernails and petal soft skin, and is irresistibly sweet when she's fast asleep.

"Could I have a few moments with just Tim?" I ask, trying to convey with the look I give everyone that I will be very upset if they say no, while keeping my voice weak, trying to retain my one big playing card of *poor me, I just had a baby, be nice.*

I'm touched when my mother links arms with Mrs Stewart without a word and leads her out. I think they might end up being friends. Maybe. Sort of.

And then, for the first time in months, I'm alone with Tim. It gives me a complete understanding of the word 'bittersweet'. I want to hold him so tightly to me that the entire security team in this hospital couldn't pull us apart. But something else - some*one* else - has to come first.

The baby makes a small noise. Tim closes his eyes, leaning his forehead on our still-clasped hands. "Hold her," I say softly.

He takes a deep breath before he opens his eyes, like he's bracing himself, or making the most of the last few moments before this all becomes real for him. She makes another little creaky noise, and he turns his head to finally look at her.

I'll remember this moment for the rest of my life.

He stands, transfixed, and just watches her for what feels like an hour but in reality is probably only a minute. Then, he reaches out his forefinger and runs his fingertip over her cheek. "What if I hurt her?" he mumbles, his voice fractured.

"You won't."

Taking me at my word, he gently reaches in, and slowly, slowly lifts her out of the glass cot and stares at her. My heart fills to overflowing as a slow, achingly happy smile spreads across his face, a single tear escaping his eye.

I bask in the moment for just a little while, trying not to let it weaken my resolve. The decision I've come to is what's right for *her*, and that's the only thing that matters. Not what my own heart is screaming and begging for.

"Tim," I say softly, and he glances at me before returning his eyes to his daughter. The bed dips slowly as he carefully sits close to me.

"She's perfect." He lifts her slowly and kisses her forehead. "You're perfect," he tells her directly. While the absolute honesty in his tone is comforting, it also twists my heart, because, although I need him to agree to this, and now know for sure that he will... God, I don't want to say what I'm about to say.

"She needs us." He looks up from his adoration, and his face starts to fall. He can see I'm serious, and that he's not going to like what's coming. "And...listen..." I take a deep breath. I had a speech prepared, but I let it go. There is no speech that can fully cover this. "We have so, *so* much growing up to do now. And... relationships...romantic ones, I mean... They can break up. They often do. But people who...stay close friends, and commit to that..." I wipe under my eyes. This is all so much, too much. I'm still shell shocked from what I've been through physically. If I'm honest with myself, I'm scared that it could happen again, which would be made more likely if Tim and I carried on our relationship the way it was.

I'm tired. I'm overwhelmed. I want someone to hold me and tell me everything's going to be OK, and lift up some of the heavy load that's settled on my shoulders. I desperately want - *need* - to be a good mother, and I want to just go home and put my feet up with a good book and have a sandwich and forget about everything for a little while.

And, more than anything, I want Tim to hold my hand through it all.

"What's her name?" he whispers.

I bite my lip, sensing that he's on board. "I don't know. What do you think we should pick?" He's been shut out of too much already; I promise myself that I'm going to agree to whatever he wants to call her.

He gives her a long, loving look. He may be young, but he's a dad now, wrapped around her little finger. "There's a song I really like. Can we name her after that?"

I lean forward a little so I can see her too, ignoring how the movement makes my vulva feel bruised. "Sure." I trust him. He won't have picked anything janky.

His answering smile is sad, but also kind of peaceful. Like he knows we're doing the right thing. "It's by Jet. It's called *Eleanor*." I think of the lyrics, and smile.

She makes a contented, comfortable little yawn, and we both manage a soft chuckle together. "Eleanor Stewart. Sounds good," I offer.

He shakes his head. "Eleanor Karas-Stewart. You deserve a mention." Our eye meet goes on just a little too long, and we rest our foreheads against each others, despairing but resolute.

"We will always be in each other's lives," I promise him, and he nods.

"I'll always love you, Nat," he whispers back, and I bury my face in his shoulder and go entirely to pieces as he recites the Walt Whitman poem he ended all his secret notes to me with. "Loved you then. Love you still. Always have. Always will."

And, for now, those words need to be enough for us both.

Chapter 6

Then

Nat and Tim are both 17

Nat

"Maaaaaaaasabadafah!" Eleanor shouts as she reaches for me, making grabby hands imperiously. Mum hands her over and ruffles her hair.

"Thanks," I tell her. She held El while I got changed for my dance class tonight. I've been able to pick it back up, and it's been great for helping me feel like myself again. And Mum's been brilliant, really solidly helping me out and giving me advice while still leaving me to make final decisions, respecting the fact that I'm Eleanor's mother. Even if I'm still not old enough to buy an alcoholic drink in a pub.

"No probs. Alright, I'm off. Tim still dropping by?" It's Mum's book club and my dance class this evening, so Tim always looks after our daughter on Thursday nights at Mum's. And yet, Mum always checks, even though he's never once been late.

"Yep." I kiss El's chubby little cheek and don't bother calling her out. Things are mostly good between us, and it's not worth it.

"OK, have a good lesson." She smiles at me and waves at El as she grabs her bag and heads out.

"Borrrrrrrrbaba," my daughter advises me sagely, and I laugh and cuddle her, spinning in a circle the way she likes until she giggles. She's just started making more recognisable sounds, trying so hard to have a proper conversation with everyone, and it melts me every single time. She's magical, and damnit, I'm glad she's here. *Even if I still have nightmares about how she arrived.*

"Would you like a banana?" I ask her.

"Nanananana," she agrees, and I carry her to the kitchen and peel it for her, holding it so she doesn't drop it. I grin when my independent little munchkin pulls my hand towards her, wanting to feed herself rather than be fed.

When she's eaten about half, the doorbell rings. I check the clock. Ten minutes to six. My heart pings; he's always a little earlier than the agreed time, soaking up every minute he can with her. "Is that Daddy?" I ask her, and she calls out, "DADAAAA!"

I open the door quickly, knowing the sort of fit she'll throw if I dawdle even a second, and beam at Tim as she lunges for him, demanding to be held.

"Heyyyy, Princess," he says warmly, and holds her close as she clutches his shirt and the strap of the bag over his shoulder. I know it's hard for him to not have her all the time, like it is for me when she spends nights with him, but we've made it work, and he's a brilliant father. Utterly devoted and all in. Nothing is too much trouble, he changes her nappies without pulling a face, and he's stayed up all night with her when she's been unwell, even if he had college the next day.

We're both continuing our education, him at the college and me at the local sixth form centre, with the help and support of our families. Cathy Stewart has become a friend, even if her husband is still gruff and sour. Even he, however, is not immune to Eleanor's gummy smiles, and he hasn't yet spoken a cross word to her. The moment he does, he's out, as far as I'm concerned. And as for Sadie... She's the best aunt anyone could wish their child to have: attentive and present, full of handmade gifts and fun vibes, and always happy to babysit if needed.

Next year is going to be interesting. And not in the best way, speaking purely selfishly. I'm going to study locally to be a dance teacher, helping others reach those heights that were nearly mine; but Tim is all set to go to a great university for his qualifications in IT. It'll almost certainly take him away from Foxton, and to be honest, I dread that. It'll confuse Eleanor, and not seeing him when she expects to will break her poor little heart.

And mine.

It may have been my idea for us to split and focus on co-parenting, but that doesn't mean I don't still love him with everything I am. And the idea of him moving away, even temporarily…maybe even moving *on*… It makes a cold pit of sick emptiness open up in my stomach. I won't be there when he goes. I know I won't be able to watch him drive away. I'd run after him, begging him to come back and stay, and that would be monumentally selfish. He's so fluid with technology, an obvious computer genius; if gardeners have green fingers, his must emit their own WiFi signal. The sheer number of times he's fixed my old PC and gotten it working when it's a hunk of irredeemable junk says it all, as far as I'm concerned. He deserves to get to the very top of his game, and I won't stand in the way of that. But then, it's not just about him *or* me anymore. We'll figure something out, visit him at the weekends or something to make sure El still has a very present Daddy.

Unless he makes other plans with someone else…

I shake it off, frowning to myself for being so unfair. Tim would never put anything above spending his time with his daughter. He hasn't yet; he even quit his spot as captain of the school football team because he'd rather read Eleanor stories and put her to bed than go to all their practices and matches. I wasn't the only person giving something up after parenthood hit.

"All good?" he asks me with a bright smile.

"Yep." I hand him the half eaten banana. "Just to let you know, the last couple of evenings she's wailed in the bathtub until you bring in Mr Unicorn to watch her do splashies."

"Alright, I'm sure we can make some sort of arrangement, hey, El?" I love the way he speaks to her, talking normally like they're having a proper conversation.

"Yoooooooocaw." She nods importantly. "Yooooocaw spash."

"Did you bring a change of shirt?"

"I brought two." He taps his bag. "After last time…"

I grimace. There was a projectile vomiting situation. It did mean I got to come home to him shirtless and trying to dry his top with my hairdryer, which was both hilarious and distractingly hot, reminding me how achy and wet he can still get me in spite of my best efforts to let that go. "Yeah, good call." I cast around for something else to say that isn't about the baby. "How… How are things? Generally, I mean."

He gives me another warm grin. "Yeah, all good. Got accepted into Foxton University."

I gape. "You did?" My brain short circuits. *He's staying.* He's going to stick around and not move away. "But…I thought your dad wanted you to go to Cambridge?"

He snorts. "Not what I wanted. And besides, there's no way I'd leave my little princess here." He kisses Eleanor's head, and she continues smushing banana into her face, unaware that her mummy's knees are weak with relief for us both.

"We could have made something work," I murmur, scratching the back of my neck. "If you'd wanted to go somewhere else…"

He grabs my wrist, and heat and longing jolts through me, emanating from his grasp. "Nat," he says quietly, "I could never leave. I'd be miserable." *Without you*, I hear in my imagination. In my deepest dreams.

My eyes meet his, and his steady, determined look tells me everything I need to know. And everything I can't bear to hear. I thought maybe the feelings I had for him would lessen in time, dial back to a manageable level, but they haven't. They won't. All that ever exists in my mind is him and our daughter, playing and giggling together, him lying on the carpet and holding her up, flying her around like superman. The way he makes up stories with kickass queens and generals, all called Eleanor, who rescue themselves rather than waiting for Prince Charming, and rule their kingdoms fairly and independently. How he's never, not once, been impatient with her, even when she's teething and fractious or just in a temper. Even when I'm not *actively* thinking of them both, they're there, in my head, the two people I love most in the whole world.

Someday, my choice won't hurt as much and won't feel so stupid.

I gently tug my wrist back. "As long as you're sure," I mutter, picking my own bag up from the counter.

"Yep. Still. *Always.*" He says the last word really quietly, and I have to go before I break down and beg him to forget what I said and come back to me.

To recalibrate, I look at Eleanor. She needs us both to be a solid and reliable unit for her, and young love is anything but. She's more important than my lingering feelings. I can do this. *For her.* "Bye, sweetie," I say, giving her a kiss. "Be good for Daddy."

"She's never anything but." He nods at the door. "Sure you don't want me to drive you?" he doesn't ask during the winter months, when it's dark outside by this time: he *insists*.

"I'm good. She's settled here now, anyway." I pull my eyes away and go to the door. "Call me if you need to."

"We'll be fine." He looks like he's about to say something, and then sighs, discarding whatever it was. "Have a great class."

We're doing the right thing, I insist to myself as I leave. *We ARE.*

My dance teacher lets me clean the studio and lock up after classes, in exchange for free lessons. It was a really kind offer I was glad to accept; the baby takes up all of my mother's spare income, and without this generosity from Mrs Shevchenkova, I don't suppose there'd be enough money to pay for them.

It also allows me a little time after everyone has left to have the studio entirely to myself. And this is *my* time. I'm not Mummy. I'm nobody's daughter. I'm not a schoolgirl. I'm just *me*. And I cut loose, dancing however I choose for a few precious minutes to whatever music strikes my fancy among the CDs in Mrs Shevchenko's collection. Sometimes I bring my own, but I don't like to plan too much.

I'm trained in ballet, jazz, tap, street dancing, samba, all sorts. But in these moments, I let the music inspire me and freestyle my butt off. I think if I didn't have these moments, I'd have given in to depression long ago. Dancing is my therapy, my touchstone, my north star. I can't put into words what it means to me.

Today I started with *Diamonds* by Rihanna, and *Die Young* by Ke$ha followed because I put a compilation album on random to keep myself on my toes. I'm in the middle of twirling around to *Some Nights* by fun. when I hear the door bang and nearly lose my balance, righting myself just in time.

"Sorry," Tim says, and I turn the music off so I can hear him better, catching my breath. "I'm...sorry I interrupted."

"Where's Eleanor?" I ask, a mother's reflex.

"Sadie's looking after her," he replies, and I relax. She's great with El, and I know she'll be safe.

All thoughts of relaxation and safety fly out of the open windows when I see the way Tim's looking at me. Like...

Heaven help me, like he *loves* me.

"I'd almost forgotten," he says hoarsely, taking slow steps towards me. "The way you dance...the way you *look* when you... Somehow, I'd really nearly forgotten."

"Why are you here?" I ask quietly. It's not that he's unwelcome. He's *never* unwelcome. But I only just about keep the way I still feel about him simmering below the surface as it is. If we're alone together, and he's looking at me like that... My resolve can only take so much, and Eleanor isn't here to remind me who we're doing this for and why it's important.

"Because I touched your wrist earlier, and my fingers are still burning from the contact," he says simply.

"Tim," I say, a water-weak warning in my voice, but it's already

61

too late.

"Look, I know," he says, stopping toe to toe with me and closing his eyes on a sigh. "I know we can't start things up again. I know you want to put that aside while she needs us, and I get it. But…" When his hands lightly touch my waist and pull me gently towards him, I make no attempt to resist for the simple reason that I can't. "But just for now, we're alone. And it's a time and space outside of everything else. It doesn't… This moment can be just for us," he finishes, and takes my mouth in the sort of starving, desperate kiss that speaks to how much restraint we've had to show to stay apart for so long. How much we've both had to sacrifice for reasons that feel very far away and not terribly significant right now.

Unable to stop myself, I wrap my arms around his neck and kiss him back with all the loneliness for him that I have ever felt. He tastes so perfectly familiar and yet just as exciting - no, *more* exciting - than the first time. My head spins, my fingertips are throbbing in time with my pulse, and the moment he cups my face, I am completely done for, and let out a moan full of all the longing and need I've been coping with until now.

In response, he lifts me up into his arms and sets me down on the pile of gym mats next to the wall, his body covering mine.

"No," I say, sitting up and pushing him away. He looks at me without any irritation, just catching his breath and giving me space. "I can't get pregnant again, I just can't, I can't go through that again, I can't do it - "

"Hey, whoah," he says gently, tucking a loose strand of hair that escaped my ponytail behind my ear. "That's not what I'm doing here." He chuckles darkly as he takes in my sceptical scowl. "No, really. I just want…" He kisses me again like he just can't resist it. "Let me make you feel good," he pleads, running a finger along the inside of my waistband. "I promise not to fuck you."

I trust him to keep to his word. And even if I didn't…I so badly want whatever he's planning to do to me that I'd be nodding my consent and lying back on these mats regardless.

He must be as ravenous for me as I am for him, because in under ten seconds, my leggings and my knickers are thrown to the side and he's wrapping my legs around his neck. He runs a few hurried kisses up my thigh before leaning forward, groaning in what sounds like ecstasy when his tongue touches my pussy. We only got to do this a handful of times back in the day, and once we both got the hang of it, it was indescribably fantastic. *I've missed this. I've dreamed of it and longed for it and came close to begging him to do it just once more, just one more time, and now here we are, thank god…*

He runs his tongue up and down my slit like it's his deepest held fantasy, over and over, until I feel like my fuse is sizzling close to its end. My back bows as I hold his head in place desperate for him to never stop, never never stop… Oh, *Christ*, the way it feels when his tongue massages my clit is going to send me crazed, and I let out a keening moan while begging him to keep going, because the feeling is building, building, *fuck I'm gonna die…*

I throw myself off the cliff willingly and eagerly, dissolving into fireworks that fizz along my veins and pull my abdomen taut. Tim lets out a hoarse noise, lapping up every last drop of my orgasm like it's his last chance.

He's not wrong.

As I come back to reality, the first tendrils of guilt reach for me. We can't allow ourselves to get derailed like this. I'm…scared. I admit that to myself at last. I'm scared to start fucking him again in case another accidental baby is created. Terrified stiff of going through it again, the needles, the blood, the puking, the unbelievable pain that still revisits me in flashbacks. And I'm scared that, if I can't offer him sex - because who knows if Eleanor was the result of withdrawal or a broken condom - he'll get bored and leave. Or the reality of being a full time parent, no days off while the other one has Eleanor, will break us somehow. Dear, darling Eleanor, the beat of my heart and the light of my life. I want better for her. I'm scared he'll leave for some reason, any reason at all, and I won't be able to survive it. It'd hurt worse than childbirth.

But for now…

I reach for the button of his jeans, but he catches his hands in mine. "I already did," he murmurs, laughing softly. "When you came, I came."

I'm torn between smugness that I have this effect on him, a surge in horniness at the thought of him helplessly blowing his load in his boxers without me even having to touch him, and sadness that I don't *get* to touch him in this precious stolen hour.

He kisses my lips, slowly and gently, and I can taste myself on his. "I'll help you clear up and lock up in a little while," he promises, "but…please can I just hold you for a bit?"

I never knew it was possible not only to glow, but to do it sadly. But how can I resist this? *And why should I?* It doesn't count, after all. *A time and space outside of everything else.* So I open my arms to him, and my heart and soul are physically aching at how *right* it feels to be wrapped up in him like this. Like home.

Like perfection.

He lifts up and peppers my face with gentle kisses. "Don't look so down," he teases. And before I can respond, his face changes. His expression morphs into one of fierce determination, narrowed eyes and steely jaw. "I heard what you said earlier, about moving on," he mutters, "and I've got to say, I'm disappointed in you." He puts a finger over my mouth when I try to answer that. "No, listen to me for a moment. Putting us on hold is the right thing to do right *now*, but one day, Eleanor will be old enough to leave home. Old enough to handle things by herself. And then…" he kisses me again, lingering because we have to stop soon, "I swear to you," *kiss,* "I'll come and get you. And you'd better be ready for me when I do, because Walt Whitman still applies here."

Chapter 7

Then

Nat is 22, Tim is 21

Nat

"It'll be OK, El," Tim says confidently, bending over to look her in the eye. Eleanor is a bit of a wreck right now; it's her first school play, and she's been practicing her part so hard the last couple of weeks. She's word perfect and could do the dance steps in her sleep, and she's been nothing but confident and enthusiastic...

...until she saw the stage all ready, and the families all filling the seats in the school hall.

"Promise?" Her lip is trembling and her eyes are huge. Her costume - she's dressed as a rabbit, a costume I spent freaking *ages* on YouTube figuring out how to make - jiggles as she hops from one foot to the other. She and the other children are in clusters backstage, and there's a heady mix of excitement and nervousness in the air.

"Promise."

"Pinky promise?" she pleads with him. I beam. That's her ultimate litmus test. If someone pinky promises her something, they'd damn well better follow through.

Tim offers her his little finger, and they shake on it. "I'll be right there, in the front row. If you get nervous, wiggle your nose at me, and I'll make funny faces until you feel better."

El giggles, reassured and a little more settled. Tim is a lot better with her worries and fears than I am. I try to logic them out with her, which doesn't seem to really make a dent, whereas he just has this knack of coming up with good workarounds and making her laugh until her confidence returns.

I remember him doing the same thing for me before I went on stage for my dance performances. Having him there, so filled with confidence in me and unabashed admiration for what I did... My goodness, it made all the difference.

I tuck my phone back in my bag. I won't remind her that we're filming this for Granny, my mother, who can't be here tonight. She's been admitted to hospital because she collapsed a couple of days ago. The cancer treatment has been rough on her, and they're keeping her in for a couple of days for observation.

Tim must notice the distracted look on my face, because he reaches out and squeezes my shoulder. "I'll record it, too," he whispers, and I smile gratefully. Mum was so upset that she couldn't be here to see it, and she made me promise over and over to film it for her. Eleanor's too young to understand what cancer is, but she knows her Granny is very poorly, and she hugged her in the hospital bed and promised to dance 'extra super awesome' for her.

"OK, everyone, it's time," Miss Yaroslaw calls to the children milling around, and they all gather to her. "OK, take your places, just like we rehearsed." El turns and waves at us, before taking her friend Jenna's hand and wandering away.

Tim and I sit next to each other in the front row with Sadie and his parents. Sadie gives me a wink, Cathy smiles warmly, and Mr Stewart deigns to give me a nod. Must be a red letter day. He does try with Eleanor, but I've had to speak up a few times when he's been a little over-demanding with her. I know he doesn't like that, but he doesn't scare me anymore.

Besides, Cathy is wonderful with her, and El hero worships her Aunt Sadie.

The play begins, a sweet story about the Easter bunny losing all his eggs the night before Easter, and the quest to find them all with his bunny friends. El's part doesn't begin until about ten minutes in, and without knowing when it happened, I realise Tim and I are clasping hands, the ones not holding our phones up. He looks as achingly proud and touched as I feel, and this moment makes everything seem worthwhile. From the lack of a social life to giving Tim up for the sake of stability… I wouldn't trade this moment, this *life*, for anything.

Eleanor tap dances with sweet little hippety hops, like the bunny she's playing, and she looks much more at ease now she's into it.

Until…

As a dancer, I know that it happens sometimes. You get wrong footed and stumble. You work hard to make sure it doesn't happen on the big night…but sometimes it just does.

El stumbles and falls to the stage floor, banging her knee. Fortunately I can tell she's not injured. But her pride is smarting and she's very embarrassed, and she looks at me and Tim with eyes swimming with tears. Her bunny face crumples as her friends carry on with the routine, and there is an audible hum of startled sympathy in the audience. Even Miss Yaroslaw looks a bit wrong-footed.

Before I can blink, Tim has dashed up onto the stage and scooped Eleanor up for a cuddle, not caring that the whole place is watching…and then…

My heart…

He encourages her to keep dancing by *copying the moves himself while holding her hand.* He's a little clumsy, but he has the basic moves down, and throws himself into pirouetting and leaping to make everyone forget El's misstep in their amusement.

"Yeah, Tim!" Sadie shouts, clapping and hooting her support. This inspires a round of applause from everyone else. Well, almost everyone else. Mr Stewart looks sour at being the only grandparent whose grandkid screwed up, followed by his son making a spectacle of himself to support her. *Miserable old fool.*

I stand up and cheer them both as the routine finishes, and I'm thrilled to bits to have been able to film this. When Eleanor is older, this will be a precious, albeit cringeworthy, memory to look back on; but the bottom line is, she will know how much her daddy had her back. How much he always will, even if that costs him a little pride.

Or maybe it hasn't. He gives her a big high five and holds her arm up like she's won a wrestling match, completely at his ease. Our eyes meet, and I'm sure I'm looking at him with all the love I feel for him, but I can't bring myself to stop.

Not this time.

Especially when it makes him smile so big.

"Dad, give it a rest," Tim bites out while we all wait for the children to come out of the changing rooms.

But of course, he doesn't let up. "I'm just saying, *she* needs to stop daydreaming when she's supposed to be performing, and bailing her out like that isn't preparing her for the real world."

"Why would - " Tim begins, scoffing, but his father cuts him off in a superior tone.

"Don't raise a spoilt girl who thinks her father will always   "

Both Sadie and I open our mouths to whirl on Mr Bastard Stewart for being so unfeeling to a six year old little girl who merely stumbled. But Tim takes a step forward towards his father and handles business by himself.

"Every *single* day," he says in a quiet, dangerous voice, "I'm so glad that I'm her father and not you. And I'll thank you to butt out and stop offering unpleasant and unwanted advice on how to make my child as miserable as you made us."

Cathy makes a choked noise as her husband goes puce. I don't think I could be more proud of Tim than I am right now. I know from before how much his father used to intimidate him; for the second time tonight, Tim is showing up for his daughter.

He may be only twenty one, but she could not possibly have a better father than Tim Stewart. I've met some other men in the past few years, and my boss's son at the Foxtrot-On-Sea Dance Studio has been incredibly nice, and made it clear that he wants to take me out. That my being a mother hasn't put him off. But nobody else will ever measure up to Tim. *Nobody*.

"Mummy!" El suddenly appears in her home clothes, her costume in a carrier bag, and throws her arms around my waist.

"Hey, sweetie," I say warmly, hugging her back and looking Mr Stewart right in the eye. "Good job, I am *so* proud of you." Her horrible grandpa's jaw tenses, but when she hugs me tighter, I know for sure this was the right thing to say.

"Ellsbells," Sadie crows, picking her up and resting her on her hip, "you did *awesome*, and I *need* you to teach me that dance."

"Really?" She sounds delighted that her hero wants to be taught by *her* for once.

"Fudge yes! And you just wait 'til I show it off to my friends. You've started a dance movement, cuddlebug." *Thank you, Sadie,* I think, and I can see the thought echoed on Tim's face.

God, I just want to throw my arms around him and kiss him. He was my first kiss, and he was amazing at it, keeping up exactly the rhythm I needed in the moment, whether that was slow and romantic or fast and passionate. He just *knew*, knew exactly how to make me feel like actual heaven was sparkling through my veins. Even when we lost our virginities to each other, clumsy and startled and hungry, he made sure that -

My phone rings, cutting through the wayward and dangerous direction of my thoughts. I wander to one side, trying to ignore how my clit has started to throb, and answer it.

"Hello, is this Natalie Karas?"

"Yes."

"Natalie, this is Sister Jeffries from Turing Ward." My heart stops. That's Mum's ward, the custom built unit for cancer patients at Foxton General. "I'm so sorry to have to tell you this, especially over the phone. Are you sitting down?"

"Uh-huh." I'm not, but I don't want to delay hearing what she has to say. Or do I?

"Are you with people?"

"Yes." *Please, just tell me…wait, don't…I mean…*

No.

"I'm afraid it's not good news. Your mother suffered what we believe to have been a heart attack. We tried to resuscitate her for around thirty minutes, but unfortunately our attempts failed, and I'm afraid she passed away a few minutes ago. I'm so sorry for your loss…"

I gag. "N…no," I cry out, and then try for a calmer voice. "No. That's not right. She was fine when I left her earlier."

"Natalie - "

"She was fine," I repeat, insisting. "She was fine. She was *fine. She was fine!*" My voice has gotten louder, more panicky, and I can't feel my legs or take a deep breath. I've got a death grip on my phone, but it's no longer held to my ear. My vision blurs with tears, and I feel familiar arms encircle me from behind, holding me upright as my knees collapse and I burst into loud sobs, still insisting, "She was fine…"

Sadie takes Eleanor for the night. Cathy offered, but I don't want my daughter around Mr Stewart in case he gives her anything even resembling a hard time about whatever stupid shit he can invent in the moment. Sadie will let her stay up late and play with her makeup and mainline sugar; and honestly, if it can help her forget the sight of her mother falling apart like that, I'm grateful for it.

Tim is driving me home after taking me to the hospital, and we're in silence because my brain is a tornado of shock, horror, and the icy fingers of early grief. He's keeping his hand locked to mine, even when he needs to change gears, and it's all that's keeping me anchored to the earth, vaguely in the here and now.

His thumb slowly, gently strokes my hand, and I let that comfort me. I need it. Need *him*. And he's there, doing what needs to be done to help me in my hour of need without asking for anything from me in return.

I'm an orphan. I don't have my mother anymore. She will never laugh with me as we make dinner, or gush over the pictures Eleanor draws for her. She's gone. Just...*gone*. Where did she go?

I knew the cancer was bad. And I knew the treatment was rough on her. She was so frail and the skin on her face was so sunken and greyish yellow. She was frighteningly bony. But somehow I just believed that she'd go through hell and come out the other side. I thought she'd recover, and then we could go back to something resembling normal. Not exactly the same - cancer would never allow that - but something close, and maybe even imbued with more gratitude than before.

Seeing her in the hospital... I keep having flashes of her in my head. Eyes, unseeing, rolled to the side. Mouth slack. Lips white. I wish they could have covered her with a sheet first, so I could have steeled myself to pull it back. Walking in and being confronted with that without any choice in the matter... It was worse.

Tim was my mouth piece when talking to the hospital staff. They were very kind, but I was too numb for much. Like the slice of a deep wound, when you know it will hurt like hell later, but right now the nerve endings aren't reacting.

But in any event, I was given some paperwork and some gentle advice, and now I'm going back to my mother's house, where I have lived for almost ten years. Now I'll be living there without her, all alone on the nights El spends with Tim. Almost everything in that house is hers. She will be everywhere, and she will be nowhere, and walking inside is going to hurt so much.

"I'm taking tomorrow off," Tim murmurs to me as he pulls up outside the house.

"No," I reply, shaking my head. He literally just started his job at the University of Foxton's IT department last week. He can't take time out now. It's too soon. He'll get into trouble.

"Yes," he says back, his tone firm. "You need me. They'll just have to understand." And with that, he gets out of the car and walks quickly around to open my door. I didn't have a chance to argue, and to be honest, I don't have it in me to do so anyway. He's crouching next to me, just waiting, letting me act in my own time without hurrying me. He's doing everything right.

He's being exactly what I need.

I hold out my hand, and he takes it without hesitating as I get out of the car. I hand him my keys, and he takes them, opening the front door, and then just waiting for me. "Take your time," he whispers.

I reach for his hand again, letting his warmth seep into my skin to give me strength and courage. I may have tears pouring down my face, but that doesn't mean I'm not brave or capable. He squeezes, and I squeeze back. My legs start moving, and I'm over the threshold.

Those are Mum's keys in the key bowl.

That's the shelf unit she painted herself nailed to the wall, covered in the Toni Raymond pottery she loved so much.

There's the photo of her hugging Eleanor at her third birthday party, her smile so huge because she loved her granddaughter so, so much...

And this is just the hallway.

I crumple for what feels like the millionth time in the past three hours, and once again Tim catches me, pulling me into his arms and holding me tightly. "I'm here," he whispers. "You've got me. And I'm not going anywhere."

I bury my face in his chest, inhaling the wonderful clean smell of him, and let it lull me into a peaceful plateau where I can just breathe and exist for a few sweet moments. His arms feel like a safe harbour while the sea of my life crashes around me. I may be cold, wet, and tired, but the rock I'm holding onto is solid and stable, and keeping me alive.

My hands run down his back, and I feel a gentle shiver run through him. He's holding his breath, or at least it feels like he is. And the heartbeat beneath my ear skips and jumps unevenly. My own joins in, speeding up a little at the implications of his body language. And the way it bleeds into my own.

He clears his throat softly, and I lift my head, my cheek moving slowly up the cotton of his shirt, until we're looking each other in the eye. There's a storm in his blue eyes, just barely leashed, and a muscle in his jaw is jumping.

I want him.

I *need* him.

He's the person I love, and there is no sense and no use in continuing to pretend otherwise.

His mouth is so close and looks so soft, and I can't imagine anything more wonderful than feeling it under mine again, and don't I deserve that? Don't I fucking *deserve* something beautiful in the shitshow of grief and sadness? Some measure of escape?

My lips get closer to his by millimetres, and then…

Mum's clock chimes in the front room, a few feet away. She inherited it from her grandmother, and now I've inherited it from her.

Mum.

Oh my god. What's wrong with me?

I take a few steps back, slipping out of his arms, and he lets me go. "I'm so sorry," I croak, my chest feeling tight. "Oh, Christ… how could I…"

He throws his arms around me again. "It's OK."

"No," I sob. "How can I be… When my mother just…" If anything, this has broken me more than anything else so far. How could I be so callous as to feel horny, to entertain the idea of kissing him and making love, when my mother isn't even cold yet? What does that make me?

Tim cups my face, his eyes full of sympathy and understanding, and not even a hint of resentment at being teased with a possibility that was then snatched away. "Don't think about that now," he orders me, kissing my forehead. "It's not important right now. I'm going to put you to bed, and I'm going to stay with you all night, and I'm going to be on top of the covers. And if you need anything at any time during the night, all you need to do is open your mouth and ask me. OK?"

I have no idea what I did to deserve him.

And I don't know how we can move past my admission.

But stability is needed now more than ever, and this time, not just for Eleanor.

For me.

Chapter 8

Now

Nat and Tim are both 30

Text thread between Eleanor Karas-Stewart and Sadie Mills:

Eleanor: Aunt Sadie... *bats eyelashes*

Sadie: Yes, Ellsbells?

Eleanor: Could you do me a favour and get me a bottle of champagne pls xoxo

Sadie: Get YOU a bottle?

Eleanor: LOLOLOL not me silly, it's for mum&dad

Eleanor: Setting an atmosphere for a romantic night in so they can bring on the luuuuurrrrrrrrrve

Sadie: Oh lol I gotchu

Sadie: Yeah, sure. Strawberries too?

Eleanor: YES OMG [heart eyes emoji]

Sadie: Drop by tomorrow, we'll have it all ready [wink emoji]

Tim

Carrying Nat upstairs when she gets home is without a doubt the highlight of my year so far.

Especially when I feel her hands clinging around my neck. "I'm heavier than the last time you carried me," she protests, and she's not wrong. Nat herself has always been feather light, with a slender dancer's frame, but both her legs are still in casts. One of them is strapped into a brace, which is even heavier.

"Dad's strong, though," Eleanor pipes up from behind us, my determined hype man. She's getting her mum's wheelchair in from the car, and our girl is practically vibrating with excitement at all three of us living in the same house for the first time.

"Yeah, but even so…" Nat gives me an uncertain look.

"You're fine," I murmur to her. "Hold on tight." *Because I can't get enough of the way you feel, back where you belong.* She wraps an arm further around my neck, and I don't resist whispering, "Good girl." Her eyes fly to mine, and I grin when I see her face going pink. I look away, but not before I notice her pupils widen.

When we get to my bedroom, she gasps a little as she takes everything in, from the snowdrops bed set to the TV. "Oh my gosh!"

"Welcome to your new home," I say lightly. If I have my way, it will be.

"You didn't have to do all this." But the way she's looking at me, like I'm her own personal hero, makes all the DIY worthwhile. Even the moment I accidentally caught my thumb with a hammer, which hurt like a sonofabitch.

Maybe I'll be able to get her to kiss it better later.

"Isn't it awesome?" El gives me a wink, and I snort. She's not subtle, but it's cute as hell. "And we've got snacks, so why don't we all settle down with a movie?"

"El," I warn her gently, "Mum might want to have a nap instead."

"No, a film sounds nice," Nat says as I lower her onto the bed.

"Great, because I've got your favourite," El sings. "*Dirty Dancing* is loaded up and ready to go." And indeed, while I was picking Nat up from the hospital, she's been busy getting things set up here: the scented candles are lit, there are chocolate chip cookies on a plate and popcorn in a bowl, and the opening credits of *Dirty Dancing* are on pause.

"That's not your mum's favourite movie," I mutter.

El frowns. "I'm pretty sure it is."

"Nope. *Tucker and Dale vs Evil.*"

We both look at her, and Nat sheepishly points to me.

"No way," El laughs, "I thought you were all about the *Hungry Eyes*! You love dance movies…"

"Well, DD is my second favourite movie," Nat says, leaning back against the new and plumped up pillows. She's still a little pale and tired, but her smile lights up her face. "I'm very happy to watch it."

"That's cool, we can watch *Tucker and Dale* first," El replies, picking up the remote and flicking through streaming services until she finds it. When her mum pats to the left of her, she stretches out by her and settles her head on Nat's shoulder. Fortunately, El has never claimed to be too old for affection, and indeed welcomes it.

Nat turns to me and nods to her right. "Settle in, if you like," she tells me, and I don't need asking twice. Looping my arm around both my girls together, I grab a cookie with my other hand and relax.

I'm not altogether surprised when Nat's head lolls into the crook of my shoulder around the time of the chainsaw bee attack scene. She's fast asleep, sighing softly, her cheek warm through my shirt.

Eleanor slowly, slowly eases away, beaming at me the entire time. "I've got some homework to do," she whispers, "so I'll leave you two alone…" She really is all in on matchmaking between me and her mother, and I hope this goes the way she wants it to. Not just for my sake, but for hers. I don't want her to feel disappointed if Nat's moved on.

Her pupils dilated when you called her a good girl, though. I feel better when I remember that. There's still *something* there on her side. And, I think, putting my arms around her and stroking her hair slowly, I can wait. I can wait here while she dozes on me so she stays comfortable, and I can wait for her to come around to the idea of us no longer smothering our feelings for each other.

I've waited literally half my life for this chance. A few more days, weeks, months, or however long she needs won't kill me.

She may be the one sleeping, but I'm the one in a dream.

The two hours Nat spends in my arms feel so right. Like I never should have stopped holding her this way. Surely she can feel it, too, given how peacefully she's napping. I'm almost sorry when she stirs, until I get to look at the beautiful warm colour of her irises again. "Mmmph, sorry," she purrs, still coming back to consciousness, and it sounds so sexy that I'm twitching in my boxers again. I didn't consider that my dick might be an issue when she moved in, that it would start stiffening on a hair trigger, and maybe I should have. "How long was I out?"

"Couple of hours," I whisper, holding her a little closer. "You can go back to sleep if you want." *I could never get tired of this.*

"Mmm-mmm," she declines, "there's something I want more than more sleep."

"Which is?"

She smiles at my shoulder. "Properly clean hair. Showering was such a mission in hospital, and the hair wash caps they give you when you can't get out of bed…they don't cut it." Looking around the room, she starts to sit up. "Where's Eleanor?"

"Doing her homework. And she'll be getting picked up for football practice in a few."

"Damnit." Nat sighs. "I forgot about practice. I'm so out of the loop."

Lightbulb moment. "I can wash your hair for you?" *Please say yes, please say yes...*

She lifts an eyebrow. "Ah, don't worry about it, I'll wait until El's home."

"Come on." I raise an eyebrow right back at her. "I can do it. It's no big deal." Except it absolutely *would* be a big deal for me, and I have to stifle a low moan at the idea of running my fingers through her hair over and over, feeling the wet silkiness and lathering it up with her go-to shampoo brand, which I've bought specially for her stay.

"Um...over the sink, right? Or the bathtub? Not in the, er, sh-shower...together, I mean..." It's so adorable the way she trails off and avoids my gaze when she realises how awkward and ridiculous she sounds right now.

"I have a shower head attachment for the bath. I'll put you on a beanbag and you can lean back." Holding my hands up, I add, "No funny business, no water fights, just clean hair the way you're craving." *Time to bring out the big guns.* "Just imagine how good it will feel to have a *really* thorough hairwash...squeaky clean strands..."

Nat giggles and lets out a comic swoon noise. "OK, OK, you convinced me."

Fuck yes. It takes a lot of willpower not to cheer out loud, but I limit myself to a nod. "OK. I'll get things set up."

There are two huge advantages to her leaning backwards to the bath while I do this.

Number one, I don't soak her with the shower head through poor aim when wetting and rinsing.

Number two, I get to watch her face and see how much she's enjoying my touch as I lather up and massage her scalp. She's biting the two corners of her lower lip, and I bet her toes are curling in her casts. Though silent, her breathing is a little erratic, held one moment and quickened the next.

As for me, I haven't been this turned on in ages, to the point that it feels like I've uncovered an unexpected kink. Hair washing. Who knew it could be so hot? But here I am with a rod as hard as steel, and I've bitten down on more groans than I do when I think of Nat while I shower. *Fuck.* Now I'm thinking about showering *with* her, watching the soap suds slide down her skin, droplets of water collecting on her nipples one at a time for me to catch with my tongue…

Oh, Jeez.

I clear my throat. "Right, I'll just rinse this off, and then I'll condition it for you."

"Wonderful. Um, I mean, thanks." There's a pillow talk quality to her voice, but it seems to be making her self-conscious, so I decide to crack a joke to ease her tension.

"Going anywhere nice on your holidays?" I ask, putting on my best hairdresser voice, and it makes her laugh. Her eyes open, and for the millionth time in our lives, our gazes hook on each other's, and it goes on for far too long for it to mean nothing.

So, once the shampoo is gone, I pick up the conditioner and run it along the thick, satiny wet lengths a bit slower than I was planning, enjoying the slip and slide of them through my fingers. Feeling bold, I step a little closer to her, not enough to touch her, but enough so that if she inched closer to me she'd feel the effect this is having on me.

Though, I think wryly when she 'innocently' rolls her shoulder and it brushes against my crotch, I must be some kind of fucking masochist. Because even that light touch sends a spine tingling throb through my cock, and makes me want more, and more, and still more. "Let it soak in for a bit, right?" I murmur, my voice husky.

"Y-yeah..."

I notice a tiny blob of conditioner on her neck. "Hold on, some escaped..." Running my finger gently over it to pick it up, I notice that her pulse is leaping, and she shivers a little at my touch.

So I do it again, craving the physical proof that I'm not alone in how badly I want this. A gruff little noise escapes from her throat, and she's holding her breath again. I go further, running my thumb over her cheek in a way that cannot be dismissed as just friendly, because fuck this. Fuck all that time we've spent holding ourselves back. El's right: we could have made it, Nat and I, if we'd stayed together. The feelings have always been cast iron strong. We've been fools. Scared, overly cautious *fucking idiots*. And it ends now.

"Tim, what - " she whispers, and the pad of my thumb finds its way to her lips. They're so soft and warm, and I feel like I'll die if I don't feel them under mine immediately, and if I don't have them wrapped around my hard-on, stroking it up and down in her wet mouth, and... God, everywhere.

I lean closer. "God, I've missed you," I whisper against her lips, the lightest touch...

"Dad!"

Nat pulls back.

"Dad, sorry, are you there?" To her credit, Eleanor does sound apologetic and awkward from the stairs. "I've got the hospital on the phone, and they need to talk to you."

For a brief moment, I close my eyes. So close, and yet so far. "OK, princess," I call back, and grab a towel to dry my hands and to hang down in front of me so I don't traumatise my daughter with my bulging crotch. Nat has gone silent, and she doesn't look at me as I leave the room. Shit, I hope this hasn't set things back for her. We were so close.

"I was just washing your mum's hair - can you rinse off the conditioner for her?" I make a show of drying my hands, for some reason, as El hands the phone over.

"Sure." She gives me a rueful look, seemingly somehow aware of her shitty timing. Or rather, Foxton General's.

"Mr Stewart?"

"Yes," I say into the phone, reminding myself that they didn't and wouldn't have deliberately torpedoed my long awaited reunion with the woman I love.

"Hi, Nurse Pritchard from Ravenston Ward. We've found Miss Karas's wallet under her bedside cupboard."

"Oh." Well, OK, I guess that's a good enough reason to call, but did it have to be right then? "Thanks, we didn't even know it was missing!"

"Oh, good, so you haven't cancelled any cards!" I can hear Nurse Pritchard smiling. "Will you be able to pick it up today?"

"Uh, yeah, sure."

"Great, I'll leave it at the front desk for you. I'll let them know to expect you."

"Brilliant, thanks so much."

I sigh, and look towards my room, where I can hear El chattering to Nat. If it hadn't been for that call…what would be happening right now? *Fuck.* An ache of longing spreads through my chest at how close we got. I don't know how I'm going to be able to recapture that moment, but I've got to. *This isn't over.* Not by a long shot.

Especially considering what I have planned for her birthday next week.

Chapter 9

Now

Nat is 31, Tim is 30

Tim

It's been four days since Nat and I had that *almost* moment in the bathroom, and each one has been filled with palpable tension. *Delicious* tension.

The way she looks at me when she thinks I can't see her...

It's breaking me in the best way. Every time she looks away, I want to pull her face back, *make* her meet my eyes...because if she does, I don't think she could hide anymore. I don't think she could stop herself from giving in to us any more than I could.

And today's the day I kick things up another notch.

Nat always used to hate that she was four months older than me, but I never gave a shit, even when I was a kid. I can tell from the rueful smiles she gives me whenever I've wished her a happy birthday across the years that she's still not crazy about it, and this morning was no exception. Still, I managed to start the day out right by giving her breakfast in bed, the way I'd always pictured doing if we were together. Of course, if things were different, I'd have woken up next to her, instead of in the spare room, and eased her awake with my tongue and fingers...

Not this birthday. Hopefully for her thirty second, though. Or, if I'm lucky, *my* thirty first.

Eleanor had to go to school, but she was full of excitement this morning. I think she prefers watching other people have their birthdays than having her own; she gets so excited watching people open their gifts, and if there's one knack our daughter has, it's for buying perfect presents for people. The t-shirt with 'I do all my own stunts' printed on the front went down a treat, and she and her mother both cooed over the yarn and crochet hooks. I know nothing about wool, but Nat was thrilled with it all, and that was lovely to watch.

She's already started making something, twisting the hook over and over in a way that looks impossibly complicated to me. I've got her set up on the bed, stacks of pillows behind her, and she's wearing a long, loose button up dress to accommodate the casts. I need to stop thinking about lifting the hem with one finger, starting at the ankle and slowly moving up, because otherwise I'm not going to be able to focus on the rest of the day. And there's some things I definitely want to make happen.

"Bye, Mum." Giving her an enthusiastic smacker on the cheek, Eleanor looks up at me. "Any chance I could grab a couple of coins for the vending machine, please?" She gives me a fairly subtle wink. Clearly, she wants a private word.

"Have a good day, sweetheart," Nat calls.

When we get to the front door, El holds out her hand with a sweet smile. Not just a pretext, then. "Alright," I say with a faux sigh, and hand her a couple of pound coins.

"Thanks, Dad," she says, giving me a brief, hard hug. "Check out what's in the fridge," she adds quietly, beaming and pleased with herself, before slipping out the front door.

With a sense of amused trepidation, I head to the kitchen, bursting out laughing when I open the fridge door. A punnet of rather luscious looking strawberries, a tub of whipping cream, and a good bottle of champagne wait patiently on the bottom shelf for the romance to kick off. I make a mental note to ask my daughter exactly *where* she managed to obtain alcohol, and head back upstairs.

I stop by the spare room and pick up the wrapped gift I have for Nat, full of heady anticipation.

My turn.

The smile she gives me when I walk in pulls an answering one from me. Given that her injuries are threatening the last thread of her career left to her - teaching children how to dance - she's kept remarkably positive, not giving in to despair. "Where there's a will, there's a way," she said to me when I gently approached the subject with her, and I know that she'll fight for a full recovery. And if that doesn't happen, she'll find a way to stay in dancing. I'm not worried about her.

I hand her my present. "One more." It's large and flat, and my insides tingle at the thought of her opening it. I spent ages putting this together last night when we'd all gone to bed, and if anything, it ramped up my feelings for her even further to do it.

"Tim," she scolds me lightly, "you've done enough. You really didn't need to buy me a present as well."

"Open it," I order her quietly. Her eyes briefly flash with enjoyment at the order, and I store that away for later, but her attention quickly returns to opening the gift. Her face lights up in a way I haven't seen in forever when the wrapping paper is off.

It's a large photo frame filled with a collage of mementos of us. Just her and me. Things I kept and treasured over the years because they were all I had left of our relationship. A run of four photo booth photos, our younger selves pulling faces, laughing, and winding up kissing because we always did. Ticket stubs from a trip to the cinema for our first date, to see *Paul*. Notes we slipped each other in class, just silly little messages and after school plans; I kept almost all of them, and this is just a selection. A polaroid of us kneeling by her mother's Christmas tree, looking so baby-faced and happy. A program cover from the time she danced the role of Kim in an amateur production of *Edward Scissorhands,* and the five star review of her performance underneath, cut from the local newspaper. It was the role that got her the place in the Sadler's Wells class. This, and a few other little things, were items I kept in a box and looked at endlessly, until last night. Now, they're hers.

Starting right now, we can make some new memories, rather than living on the fragments of before.

"You..." She gapes at it, trying to take it all in. "That's... Oh, *Tim.*" Her eyes are wet as she smiles. "It's *us.*"

"All we were," I agree, settling on the bed next to her and looking it over with fresh eyes now she's seen it. "But not all we're gonna be," I mutter.

Her face jerks towards me, and I decide to back off. I've planted the seed. It'll be good for it to sit there for a bit. "So, what do you want to do today? Birthday girl's choice."

It takes her a few moments to reply, and when she does, her voice is a little husky, clogged with emotion. "Um... Don't you have to go to work?"

"No. I took the day off." I was allowed some time off to look after her, but I've had to go in here and there to accommodate it. Today, however, I've booked as leave.

She visibly melts a little. "Oh. Thanks." She casts around the room for ideas. "To be honest...I was planning on hunkering down with a box set. And I was going to ask you to bring some snacks up before you left. But since you're not leaving…"

I grin, and hand her the remote. "Sounds perfect. What are we watching?"

She takes it, biting her lip. *That's my job.* "Well, I actually haven't seen *Rivals* yet, but we can watch something else - "

"You haven't seen it yet? But you *love* Jilly Cooper…" I smirk. "And David Tennant, come to that." It's true. He was my *rival*, pun not intended, for her affections when we were younger. And probably still is.

"Just haven't gotten around to it yet."

Perfect. I've already seen it, and I know what happens in the very first scene. Am I a bit evil? Maybe. But I can't resist the idea of watching it with her. "Then let's do it."

And, sure enough, in the first three seconds we see an actor's clenching buttocks as he joyfully thrusts into his partner, who cries out in ecstasy as they join the mile high club. The scene is shot comically and in the spirit of fun, but the raw sexuality is inescapable. I chuckle when Nat goes bright red and covers her face with one hand. "Oh *shit*… I didn't think…"

I give her a look. "It's listed as a 'bonkbuster'. Scenes like that can't come as a surprise to you."

"Yeah, but…it hasn't even started yet…" She cringes as the woman's cries take on a climactic quality. "Bloody hell."

"Hey." I take her wrist and gently tug it away from her face. "We're both adults. There's nothing wrong with watching, and *enjoying*, some adult content." *Is your pussy feeling fluttery, Nat?* Even the idea has me starting to harden.

"Right." She sighs, and joins me in a laugh. "I'm being ridiculous."

I tip my head to one side. "We are, you know."

"What?"

"We're both *adults*." The meaning in the look I give her surely can't be brushed off. "We're not kids anymore, Nat."

She presses her lips together, and I feel a twist of disappointment when she looks away, back to the posh twats baiting each other on the plane. But then she whispers, "I know."

I can't concentrate on this damn show. I enjoyed it when I first saw it, but the woman I love, have always loved, is next to me on my bed. Her side touches mine here and there, and I can smell her perfume. White Musk by The Body Shop. She wore it then, and she wears it to this day. It filled my senses when I lost my virginity to her, and it has me slavering inside like Pavlov's dog now it's so close. The memories of her underneath me, the way she made sweet little gasping noises when I eased my cock into her, breaching her. Burying my face in her neck and breathing in that fucking gorgeous floral scent. The tightness of her clamped around me, too much to handle, too good to be real...

The naked tennis scene follows fairly swiftly, and by that point, I'm achingly hard, twitching further when I see her thighs are squeezing together above her casts. Once again, Nat is biting down hard on her lip, and I remember how that mouth of hers tastes, and I can't wait another second to have that again.

She looks at me as though she can't not, and in perfect unison, she and I both say, "Fuck it."

Great minds.

I lean forward, and she welcomes me, holding a fistful of hair at the back of my head to keep me in place as our lips *finally* reunite, and she tastes every bit as wonderful as I remember. I can't hold back a groan of relief and satisfaction at kissing her again at last, and being kissed back, as hungrily and desperately as I am. Careful not to bother her lower legs, I roll and place my knees either side of her thighs, holding myself up so I don't squash her, and bracket her jaw with my hands. She's not going anywhere. Nothing and no-one is going to interrupt us this time.

I kiss her again, deeper, and when I seek her tongue with mine, everything between us, all the years of repressing and pretending to just be friends and co-parents and nothing more, all blow up until they're smears on the walls. She clings to me, hard, and my right hand travels down her neck, over her collarbone -

"I can't," she bursts out, pushing me back. The shock of returning to reality has my head whirling for a second or two, but the sight of her resting her forehead on her hand speeds up the process. "I'm sorry."

I try to calm down my panting and think a bit more clearly. "Did I do something wrong?"

"No," she says instantly, shaking her head hard. "No, this is a me thing."

I gently tuck a strand of her hair away from her beautiful face. Her lips are puffy, her face flushed, her eyes glittering. *God, she's perfection.* "Nat...we're allowed to do this. We're two consenting adults," I say carefully.

"I know." An impatient noise escapes the back of my throat. "I just can't...if we..." She huffs out a sigh. "I can't get pregnant again."

I laugh in relief. "I wasn't planning on doing that," I assure her. "Besides, with your legs - "

"No, I mean..." Her eyes fill with tears. "Not ever."

I nod. "OK." It may have been nice to have another baby together as adults, but I'm not wedded to the idea. I'd rather be with her, on any terms she cares to name. She's more important to me than having another El.

"You don't understand." She can't even look at me. I frown. This is fucking *serious*. "There's only one way to be safe, and that's to...*not*. I don't trust condoms, they did *nothing* for us before. And look at what happened to Sadie. She conceived Rhiannon when she was on the *implant*. So I can't trust other forms of contraception, either. My brain just won't let me." Her fingers rub her temples. "And maybe I'm being ridiculous, but you don't know what it was like, being pregnant - the sickness, the pain, the *birth*. Like being taken over and then ripped in two." Fuck, she looks almost green. "I have nightmares sometimes, that I'm fifteen again, and everyone is judging me and nobody is helping - "

"Nat." Finally, she looks me in the eye, and I take her chin in my hand. "You were fifteen years old. It was a lot for anyone to have to cope with, and you were much too young for all of it. Of course you wanted some safety and steady ground afterwards." I pause, thinking how to phrase this next part well. "Didn't you ever get any therapy? Afterwards, maybe? I always thought you might've."

"No."

I flinch. "Why not?"

"Nobody offered." She shrugs miserably. "And once Eleanor was born, it was like I should have been over it, and focusing on her, instead of getting all panicky about things that had already happened."

I feel sick, thinking of her pushing the obvious trauma all the way down so it didn't inconvenience anyone. It's as though a small part of her is still that scared, pregnant teenager, the memory of the fear and the extreme physical intensity sticking to her like a barnacle.

She lifts the remote and presses pause. "I'm sorry. I can only... I'm sorry." A tear trails down her cheek, and I can feel it running over the surface of my heart. "I understand if you don't want to take this any further. It's...not exactly an appealing prospect, a sexless relationship. But - "

"Natalie Karas." I put my hands where her neck meets her shoulders and give her a soft shake. "Is that all?"

"What do you mean, 'all'?" Her mouth curls with incredulity. "You can't be - "

"Never mind all that, just look at me." I wait, patiently, not moving or saying anything further until her eyes meet mine again. "I love you." It's a relief to finally say it again. "I've always loved you, ever since we were teenagers. I haven't let up for a single second, and it's withstood not being with you for half my life. It's not giving up now. It's not giving up *ever*." Her lower lip starts to tremble, and I capture it between my own to make her believe what I'm saying. "So that's the bedrock we're dealing with, and believe me when I say it's solid as concrete. Now, we can explore options. I can have a vasectomy, that's no problem. I'll schedule one tomorrow. But if you'd feel better just never having sex ever again, and that's the trade-off I need to make to be with you, then I'll take it."

She stares at me, and I return her look evenly. I'm deadly serious, and she needs to accept that. "You can't mean it."

"I can and I do. Nat... You're all I ever think about. All I've wanted for so long. Don't you know by now that I'd do literally anything for you?" I kiss the corner of her mouth, an idea lighting me up from inside. "Besides, there's other stuff we can do that couldn't possibly result in pregnancy."

I know I've got her when a yearning expression fills her eyes. She knows exactly what I'm talking about; all the furtive touches we tried so hard to sate ourselves with before we went all the way. But, now that they're on the table again, they'll satisfy me just fine until I get the snip. They're more than I would otherwise have, and a starving man doesn't complain if he's given bread instead of a sandwich, I think wryly.

"Let me remind you," I whisper, inwardly frantic for her to say yes, nuzzling her nose with mine. Our lips slip together, finding each other inexorably, and she nods her consent, as incapable as I am of resisting what's still between us.

I'm so grateful that her dress has buttons all the way down. They're easy to undo, and my eyes light up when I see she's not wearing underwear. Whether by necessity or by design on her part, it's a total gift. "Bad girl," I tease, and start to kiss my way down her neck. Her body is beautiful, and a little different from how I remember. She was almost flat chested before she got pregnant, and self-conscious about it, but I found her body to be ecstatically wonderful. Now, I can see how motherhood gave her gentle curves and darkened her nipples to a gorgeous dusky colour. I can't wait to roll my tongue over them, taste her skin, move lower...

"If you think it's going to be all about me again, you've got another think coming," she murmurs. I lift my head, and she's grinning at me. "That time at the dance studio?" My pulse jumps as I remember. "I didn't get to touch you, and I'm not missing out this time."

I lift an eyebrow. "Is that so..."

She nods. "Strip. You have way too much on."

What my girl wants, my girl gets. I shuck off my t-shirt and stand to discard my grey tracksuit bottoms and my boxers both together. "I don't think I've ever gotten naked so fast before." I shake my head and huff out a laugh.

Her lips twitch, running her eyes over my bare body. I wonder how much I've changed over the years, what differences *she* could have noticed. "You weren't far off during our first time."

"Could you blame me?" I climb back on top of her, as I was. "I was only a teenage boy, and you were gonna - *Jesus...*" She reaches down and grabs me, and it's the first time a hand other than my own has touched my rod in far too long. I have to fight for control, clenching my fists tight enough to hurt, to keep from spilling onto her stomach too soon. "Hang on a minute, honey," I tell her, chuckling and holding her hand still when she starts to rub me.

"I haven't started yet." She pouts, but there's mischief in it. I haven't experienced confident, playful Nat like this before. It's thrilling.

I dip my head lower, kissing down her abdomen towards her slit, but she pulls my hair to stop me. "If you're gonna do that to me, I'm gonna do that to you," she insists.

Now that *sounds fun.* "Seems fair."

A few shifts and some repositioning later, and we're in a careful sixty nine position with me on top. And I can't work out what's a bigger distraction: the delicious taste and smell of her pussy, or how dizzyingly amazing her mouth feels on my shaft. I'm on a knife edge here, and it's only been minutes. *Sue me, it's been forever.* I've got to be merciless on her, or I'll come first, and that is just not something I'll allow myself.

Her clit is so hard and swollen that I know I have a fighting chance. And I know she used to like it rubbed and licked side to side, so I do that until I hear her moaning around my cock. Unfortunately, that pushes me too close to the edge for comfort, so I withdraw for a few moments to recover, even though my dick is screaming at me to get back inside her mouth *right now*. Little minx doesn't help matters by stroking me, her grip tight and perfect, and *shit*, I'm seeing stars.

Frantic now, because I know I'm going to blow any second, I give up and start sucking on her clit like my life depends on it. Her hips start bucking as much as they can, given the casts and her position, and I hold them tightly, pinning her down and forcing her to take it, take the same electrifying pleasure she's giving me as she resumes sucking me off, let this make her clench her teeth until they crack just like me...

Fuck. I didn't ask her where she wanted me to come.

Rubbing her clit to keep her momentum up, I try to pull out again. "I'm too close," I pant, and she grabs my arse and pulls me back, sucking me deeper, *Christ*, I'm hitting the back of her throat...

I'm a goner.

I'm pretty sure I got her there at the same point I detonated, or very close. But there's a unique, damn near glorious magic in being able to taste her orgasm at the same time as feeling my own pumping out of me and into her mouth.

It's nothing short of heaven.

"Now do you believe me," I say to her, switching around so I can hold her.

"Can't not," she mutters, her voice hoarse because of me.

I smile, kissing the top of her head. "Better than *Rivals*?"

I feel her grin against my bare chest, and she looks up, resting her chin on her hand. "Yep."

There's still a shadow in her eyes, but I'm not worried. I'll call my doctor to book my vasectomy first thing tomorrow morning. It'll put her mind at rest, and that's all that matters to me, now and always.

Whatever it takes.

"Fancy some strawberries?"

Chapter 10

Now

Nat is 31, Tim is 30

Tim

Three months later

Tonight's the night.

It's been twelve weeks since my vasectomy, and I got the all clear from my doctor this morning. No more bullets in the gun. I am good to go.

Thank god, because Nat and I have been counting the days. She's been so grateful to me for doing this for her, and she really needn't. We've done the parenting thing: now, we get to spend the rest of our lives being *us.* I mean, was the vasectomy procedure the best fun I've ever had? No. But it was also no big deal. A local anaesthetic and twenty minutes of my time, and bingo. Nothing to write home about, and I was back at work the next day.

And this evening, once we've come home from the date I have planned, it becomes fully worth it.

"Am I dressed appropriately?" Nat asks me, giving me a twirl in her daisy print cotton dress and denim jacket.

"Yes. And you look beautiful," I add, kissing along her jaw until my lips meet hers.

"Gross," Eleanor pipes up as she passes us in the hallway on her way to the kitchen. The happy grin on her face takes the sincerity out of her smartarse comment. Nat and I have been discreet, but very obviously together over the past three months, and she's thrilled to pieces by this development. My ears are still ringing from her whoops of glee when we told her.

"Sorry, not sorry," Nat tells her, hugging me openly. "How's revising going?"

El makes a face. "Like a snail with arthritis trying to cross the road."

"Sounds like you're gonna pass English with that kind of turn of phrase." I smile at her sympathetically. I remember the days when I was trying to pass my GCSEs. "At least you don't have a screaming baby in the background while you memorise the periodic table."

Our daughter rolls her eyes. "Yeah, I know, you had to change nappies by the time you were my age, blah blah blah…" I ruffle her hair, and she ducks, opening her bag of popcorn and throwing a few kernels at me. "You going to Teagan's tonight?"

She nods. "Yeah. Jenna will be there, too."

"And you're gonna study, right?" I put on my best Strict Father voice, but I can't keep a straight face.

With a sardonic look, she quips back, "No, we're going to have an orgy with the boy's rugby team. I've got a bag full of condoms, and Teagan's bringing the weed."

A tiny part of me starts having an anxiety attack, even though I know she's joking, until Nat snorts with laughter. "OK, who's bringing the porno DVDs?"

"DVDs? How old are you?" El pokes her tongue out. "There are free websites for that."

Nat pulls her into a cuddle, kissing her cheek loudly and rubbing her back. "Have a great time, Toots."

"And maybe have your next study sleepover here," I add faux-sternly.

"Not happening. Teagan thinks you're hot, and it's weird." She grabs her rucksack and slips on her Converse; Teagan lives two doors down, so El doesn't need a ride. "Laterz potaterz. Have a lovebird-tacular night."

I gape at Nat when El's gone. "Um...yikes?" Nat is doubled over with laughter. "Stop, I'm...ugh. That is not information I needed."

"Have you seriously only just realised?" She's still laughing as she hugs me. "The way her friends look at you is just *blatant.*" Her eyelashes flutter, and she smirks. "You're the youngest, hottest dad they know. Of *course* they have crushes on you."

I shudder. "Could have lived the rest of my life quite happily without ever knowing that." Time for a subject change, I think as I give her a peck on the lips. "You ready to go?"

"Just need to put my lip gloss on."

"Don't bother, I'm only gonna kiss it off." She beams at me, her nose wrinkling in a way that makes my insides dissolve happily, and we head out.

I took her to the fair, which was back in town for its yearly visit just in time for my plan. We were supposed to go back when we were teenagers, but that went to hell when we found out she was pregnant. We've taken Eleanor there in years gone past as a family, including our parents, but never just the two of us.

And, as can be said about many things for us, *it's time*.

She's lit up brighter than all the fairground lights as she takes in the bells and whistles, the smell of the fresh cinnamon doughnuts and popcorn, the colours and the echoing nineties music. Huge soft toys are hanging from this one stall, and I make a mental note to win her the purple elephant. She loves elephants.

But…first thing's first.

"Ferris wheel first?" I offer, loving the way she snuggles in with my arm slung around my shoulder, holding her hand. We're three months into making up for lost time, and I still feel like a loved up teenager with her. In the absence of being able to have sex, every touch, every lingering moment, is loaded with yearning and power. It's fricking incredible, but I still can't wait for tonight. We'd be fucking right now, except I wanted her to have this. I always regretted not taking her to the fair, not telling our families to go fuck themselves and let us enjoy being young and in love for one last evening before life got real.

No more regrets.

And no more holding back.

"Sure." She looks at the ghost train and shudders. "Definitely not that ride, though."

"But the ferris wheel is OK?" I tease her.

"It doesn't have jump scares, so I'm all for it." She grins. "And besides, it'll be just the two of us."

So we queue up and I pay the teenager at the stall, and then we take our seat. I'm glad she said yes to doing this one first, because I can't wait to say what I need to say to her. I don't think I could hold it in too much longer anyway, and I want to do this right.

We kiss all the way up, laughing together every time the seats swing, focused only on each other and, occasionally, the view. Foxton-on-Sea looks incredible from this angle, with the ocean stretching out as far as the eye can see, the pier dotting lights along the front, and the brightly coloured terraced houses glowing in the twilight. It's sure as shit a romantic setting.

It takes a little while - this isn't a small wheel - but we reach the top. The moment is here. So I take a quiet steadying breath and turn to her...

...and she wriggles out of her jacket and lays it over my lap, eyes sparkling with mischief. "Let's have some fun," she whispers against my lips, unzipping my fly under the jecket and reaching inside, grabbing my cock. I had a semi from all the kissing on the way up, but it leaps into action at her touch, the throb making me gasp. These days, a few firm strokes and I'm hers for the taking. *God, that feels GOOD...*

"Whoah, wait a second," I say with the last of my restraint. Got to do the thing first.

Oh, shit, she's bending her head…

I let out a strangled groan at the touch of her tongue on my helmet. I can't think when she does that; all I can do is helplessly, mindlessly enjoy it. *No.* Must… "Nat, wait just a second - "

"It's OK," she murmurs, still in playful kitten mode, "no-one can see us."

"Yeah, but - "

"And you'll have plenty left for me later, when we get home."

"Of course, but I'm trying to - "

"So," she purrs, rubbing my shaft with the exact grip I like, rolling her thumb over the tip so the pre-cum glides over it in the most knee-trembling way, "you can just sit and *enjoy the ride -* "

"Nat, will you marry me!" It's not even a question at this point. I just blurt it out, because I know if I don't, I'll lose this perfect position on the ferris wheel and end up nothing more than a slave to her mouth. And I so wanted to propose here.

Now I've done it, though, I feel like maybe I should have had a plan B, because she's frozen in place, staring at me. "Wait, what?"

I sigh, a small smile pulling at the corners of my mouth. "I… brought you up here to ask you to be my wife," I admit, and she lets go of my dick like it's hot. I burst out laughing, and she slaps my arm.

"That's not something to joke about," she grumbles.

"Who's joking?" I turn to face her as much as I can in this seat, which swings fitfully. "Nat, what did I always write at the end of

Still

those notes I sent you while you were pregnant?"

She smiles. "'Loved you then, love you still...'"

"Always have, and always will," I finish off firmly. "I'm not kidding. I'm not wasting any more time. I've wanted to be yours since you turned up in my form room as the new girl. I have never stopped. And I'll give you fair warning, if you say yes to this, I'm frogmarching you to Vegas or Gretna Green or wherever we can get married soonest. Because I fucking love you, and... Jesus, I had a speech all set to go, and I'm screwing this up, but - "

She cuts me off with a kiss, calming down my ramble. "Ask me again," she says, her forehead against mine, her happy sniffles filling me with pure, unfiltered happiness, because she's going to say yes.

"Will you marry me?" I oblige.

"Yes," she says, barely a split second after I finish the sentence.

Natalie Karas always gives me the best moments of my life. My first kiss. My first time. The gift that is our daughter. And now saying yes to being my wife.

"SHE SAID YES!" I yell out, and a bunch of strangers on the same ride as us whistle and applaud. And I just kiss her until the ride manager laughingly taps me on the shoulder and tells us we need to get off.

He's not wrong.

107

Nat

Hand in hand, we dash back to the car as quickly as I'm able. We can come back to the fair tomorrow night. What we can't do is wait another second to go to bed together.

We can't even keep our hands off each other while he drives, him grasping my thigh and sliding his fingers closer and closer to my core, me continuing what I started on the ferris wheel by groping his crotch shamelessly. He's so intoxicatingly hard that I can't stop touching it, marvelling as it thuds like a pulse in my hand. He makes muffled groaning noises, upping the ante by rubbing my clit through my clothes.

So by the time we stumble through the front door, we're rabid, ravenous for each other and rolling along the walls as we rip at each other's clothes. I don't know which way is up, and I don't think I care; as long as he's pressed up against me, kissing me breathless, I don't care if I'm on the ceiling or upside down.

I wore my best purple lace bra and knickers for tonight, in anticipation of what we're doing right now. Ever since he had the vasectomy, I've been desperate for this moment. I want him so badly that my vulva has been aching for weeks. Fooling around has been fun, but nothing compares to this.

It's even better than I remembered.

I'm not sure how we did it, but we make it to the bedroom - *our* bedroom, since my birthday - and pull off the rest of our clothes, in a hurry to be naked together. His body is harder and more toned than when we were teenagers, and when he was still playing football at school he was in great shape. So seeing him like this is like a wink from the universe that I didn't overblow any of it in my head. I have some faded stretch marks from pregnancy that make me a little self-conscious, but, judging from the tortured noises he makes as he pins me to the bed, running his hands all over me and keeping his lips glued to my skin, I have nothing to worry about on that score.

I wrap my legs around his waist, and, within seconds, the head of his cock slips against my pussy and finds its way to my entrance. I want this so badly, and I watch, thrilled, as his skin breaks out in goosebumps and he makes a helpless, desperate noise in the crook of my neck. "Please," he begs, and gasps as I cant my hips to let him in. I feel about for his hand, and we both clutch hard, lacing our fingers together as he slides all the way in.

Ouch. It's been such a long time since I did this, and he's so very *very* hard, that I feel almost like a virgin again. But that soon gives way to blissful friction, the gorgeous and almost unbearable intensity of fizzing pleasure spreading outwards from where we're joined. I'm so wet and so powerfully turned on that every stroke of his cock inside me is like being hooked up to mains electricity.

"I've missed this," I whisper in his ear. My god, did I ever. And to be able to do this, *without a condom*, and knowing that I'm safe and he won't get me pregnant...feels like the ultimate life hack.

"Me too," he manages, looking down at me his eyes glazed. His hips jerk fitfully, and he fights for control over his movements. "And I'll never let anything keep us apart again." Finally, he settles into a hard, punishing rhythm that has me seeing stars. "You," *thrust*, "are," *thrust*, "*mine*," he insists as he fucks me, and I nod, because I am. Entirely. Neither of us are able to stop moving with each other, and when he dips his head to gently suck on my nipple, I can't take anymore. My orgasm is so sharp that it feels like I'm being pulled by the clit, and I feel a helpless scream tearing from me as my vision whites out.

"Fuck," he shouts through gritted teeth, "oh, *fuck…uhhhhhhhh,* I love you…" He continues babbling words of love to me as he pumps all those years of pain and longing and need into me, coming so hard and so much that I can feel the warmth of it spreading deep inside myself.

He puts all his weight on his forearms so he doesn't crush me, and for a few seconds we kiss lazily, breathing in each other's air. Then, before I know what's happening, he flips me over so fast I squeak, wasting no time before he starts running kisses down my spine. I can feel him, still hard, trailing down my leg as he goes. "Again?" I giggle.

"Oh, I'm nowhere near done with you yet," he rumbles darkly, pulling me up on my knees and pushing my shoulders down. My butt is in the air, and he eats me from behind like he's still starved.

"Holy shit," I gasp, driven almost crazed by the lightning-and-fireworks feeling spreading over my vulva at his tongue's swipes and tickles. "How come it's even better this way?"

He slaps my arse, and the sound gets me as hot as the stinging sensation. "I can taste us both," he confides in a low voice, and that thought has me moaning and pushing harder against his tongue as he uses it to fuck me. This feels so filthy, and after depriving ourselves of exploring each other for so long, the bliss is unparalleled, sharper and sweeter and building so fast I can hardly -

Just at the second before I go over the edge, he straightens up and slams his cock into me, all the way all at once. It hurts, but it's a good hurt, and if anything pushes me even closer to release, so close that the distance between me and heaven is paper thin. And then he pulls all the way out, before pulling me back into him and pushing into me hard at the same time. Over and over. It's so intense that, this time, my scream is silent as he shoves me into the most extreme orgasm of my life. I think what he was doing must have affected him the same way, because he can't manage words as he comes. He just shouts out.

Tim. My Tim. The affection I feel for this man is overwhelming in this moment, and he only exacerbates things when he lies next to me, gazing at me like I'm the most beautiful and precious thing in the world while he smooths my hair behind my ear. Dotting kisses along his shoulder, I grin so hard it hurts at the thought of being able to do this every night for the rest of our lives. As long as we keep it down when Eleanor's home.

I can't wait to see her face when I tell her that her mother and father are getting married. We may have gotten things a bit skewed - getting together, then having a baby, then getting together again, and *then* getting married - but better late than never.

"Then," he mutters, lifting his head and kissing me with a soft, sleepy mouth, "still...and always."

I grin. "Can we get that tattooed on our arms, maybe? To commemorate our engagement?"

"I'm up for that. Maybe we can call in to Wishbone after we've been ring shopping."

"Deal."

Epilogue

Now

Eleanor is 16

From her diary entry of 30th July:

Sorry for being a day late with this, Diary, but Mum and Dad got married yesterday, so I've been super busy. I was Mum's maid of honour, which was cool, especially since they let me pick my own dress. Disturbia. Black. Lots of belts and studs. It was COOL. I even got to have a couple of neon purple extensions put in, AND some new Newrocks platform boots. I felt like a goth princess. And they looked pretty alright too. Mum wore a blue dress that made the most of her teeny little waist, and I'm glad the wedding was small enough so that I had an excuse not to invite Teagan because she'd have been drooling all over the place when she saw Dad in a suit, and it would have been *hideous*

They don't know it yet, but I've clubbed together with Aunt Sadie and Uncle Leo to send them on an awesome honeymoon to next year's Rio Carnival. Mum will love the dancing, and Dad will love watching Mum be so happy.

The wedding was pretty sweet. They wanted to get married basically straight away, but then they realised I was still in the middle of my GCSEs, AND it was almost my birthday. And besides, there's all sorts of shit to do, like paperwork or whatever, before you can do the deed. So they waited until I was done, and my sweet sixteen birthday party had been and gone, and all their Is had been dotted and all their Ts had been crossed with the registrar people. It was a quick ceremony, but like they keep saying, they've waited long enough.

Grandad wasn't there. Can't say I miss him.

Grandma was, though, and that's awesome because she seems to have a new boyfriend. I'm just stifling down my barf at it being my old PE teacher, Mr Hartwell. Still, at least it wasn't the headmaster. He looks too much like an elderly Boris Johnson for that idea to be at all tolerable. Mr Hartwell would probably be played by Harrison Ford in the movie version of his life, and I love that for Grandma. They're so cute and affectionate it's gross, like Mum and Dad, but she's happy for the first time in freaking aaaaaages.

I missed Nana today. I hadn't thought about her in a while. She'd have been really happy for Mum, I know it.

I'm still kind of pissed that they basically could have been married all this time, but at least they're together now. They make perfect sense together. Mum moves, Dad moves. Dad laughs, Mum laughs. They're basically soulmates, and I know what I'll be looking for when my time comes.

If only Eli Gastright wasn't already married. He is fine as fricking frick. But Emily's nice, so I can't be too mad about it.

I just wish someone like him existed at my school. But all the boys in my year are exactly that: boys. Juvenile and boring and tedious. All the conversational skills of a squirrel with concussion. I feel sooooooooo ready for someone better. Someone a bit older, but not like disgusting older. Someone with a little more class, and something interesting to say. And a butt like Eli's. That'd be awesome.

When's it gonna be my turn, though?

THE END

Bonus:

A selection of Tim's letters to Nat

Dear Nat,

I'm writing this to you in English class, trying to ignore the similarities between you, me, Romeo, and Juliet. At least we're going to do better than those idiots.

Holding you today after such a long time apart was SO amazing. I'm sorry it was in the boy's toilets, but it was the best I could do at the time. But we could have been in the middle of The Bog of Eternal Stench from Labyrinth and as long as you were there it would have been incredible.

Just as incredible as it was feeling the baby kick.

I'm so sorry I've done this to you, but also, feeling that kid move inside you was just amazing. Kind of brought it home to me that you have a little person inside you, not just a thing. A thing I've been angry with for keeping us apart, but it's not his or her fault at all. Please rub your bump for me and tell them I'm sorry, and although I'm just a stupid lad, I'll be there for them every single day for the rest of my life.

And that goes for you, too.

There's a poem we're studying after R&J is done, and I've read ahead and checked out some more of his stuff. His name is Walt Whitman, and this one he wrote reminds me of us:

Loved you then

Love you still

Always have

Always will

Your Tim xxxxxxxxx

My Nattie,

It was torture before, when I was seeing you in school but not being allowed to go anywhere near you.

But it's infinitely worse not seeing you at all.

I know you have to stay at home now, because it's getting so close to the time when the baby will be born, but I just want you to know I miss you. I miss the hell out of you, and it's making my chest ache.

I've been reading up on what's going to happen and what you're going through physically. The website I looked at this morning told me that our baby is the size of a pineapple right now. Hope he or she doesn't come out feeling like one, LOL. Sorry. I shouldn't be joking. It says the baby can turn their head and can see and hear. Please tell them I love them already, and I promise you I will learn how to look after a baby properly. I'm not much, but I'll always do my best for you both. You're not alone. I will <u>never</u> let you be alone.

Loved you then

Love you still

Always have

Always will

Your Tim xxxxxxxxx

My Nat,

This year has been amazing.

I can't believe Eleanor's been with us for a whole year. In some ways it feels like she got here twelve years ago. Sometimes it still feels like twelve hours. But each and every day has been unbelievable in its own way.

And every time we do the El Handover, I can see everything that I'm feeling in your eyes. I'm exhausted; so are you. I'm knocked sideways by being a parent; you're right there with me. I'm beside myself with how much I love our daughter; you match me punch for punch with that.

I don't think my brain is big enough to process how much I adore her. The way she thinks ducks are the most hilarious thing ever. How she used to stroke my arm when I gave her a bottle. How unbelievably cute she looks when she's asleep, eyelids like petals. She's exhausting and terrifying and the best little person in the world, and the greatest gift I've ever had. I'll always thank you for her every chance I get.

I miss you, though. I know we've barely got the bandwidth for anything beyond being Mummy and Daddy and trying to get the best education we can so we can provide for her, but I do still wish we could be more again. And that I could have one on one time with you, just the two of us.

Even so_ If I got that, I know I'd miss my little best friend who looks so much like you that it makes me physically hurt sometimes, in the best way.

As ever:

Loved you then

Love you still

Always have

Always will.

Your Tim xxxxxxxxx

Nat,

I fucked up. I really fucked up badly. And I'm so sorry. I couldn't be more sorry, and I wish I could talk to you about this so I could beg your forgiveness. Forgiveness I don't deserve, even if I don't technically have anything to feel guilty for. Technicalities are where the lowlifes hide, though.

I know I'm not going to send this to you, but every time I think about what I did tonight I want to throw up, and I'll never get to sleep tonight or any other night if I don't just get this out of my head.

I was mad at you. It's no excuse, and I wasn't being reasonable, but that's at the root of it all. Our daughter's fourth birthday party, and we were all together as a family, and I'd been looking forward to it all month because I get to be with my two favourite girls for a whole day. And it was great, as I knew it would be.

Until you hugged that guy, Dimitri or whatever his name was.

Just thinking about it has my flesh on a rolling boil. I know he's your boss's son at the studio, and I know you'd have told me if he'd become anything more to you. And he was good to Eleanor, which is all that really matters at the end of the day. She was clearly comfortable with him.

But the way you hugged him so easily, and for longer than you ever do with me. You let him have something I'd kill for, something I sit up at night dreaming about, and you did it so casually. I'm only allowed to give you the briefest hugs before you step away. You back off fast if I so much as brush your arm in passing with mine, and it_hurts.

So I wasn't in the best frame of mind when I went to Mo's house party.

They do this every Saturday night, and I hadn't gone to one before. I'm not in student digs and my lifestyle is different to my classmates', but they keep inviting me anyway, and tonight I gave in because I thought a few beers with some friends would help.

And when Lila from my AI course started sitting in my lap and playing with my hair, I didn't push her off.

I didn't turn her down when she asked me to team up with her for beer pong.

I let her hug me when we won. For longer than you hugged Dimitri.

And when she kissed me_

I'm sorry, Nat. I kissed her back.

And that's not the worst part.

I kept telling myself when she was pulling me back to her on-campus dorm that I owed you nothing. (Not true; I owe you everything.) That's we're not even together, so this wasn't infidelity of any kind. And, god help me, I've been lonely, watching my classmates have the sort of easy and fun life I thought we were gonna have. I've been hungry for human contact for such a long time now, and I know that sounds pathetic but I can't help that it's true. So I told myself that, since you were free to sleep with Dimitri, if that's what you wanted, therefore I could sleep with Lila, guilt free.

Except it wasn't guilt free.

All I could think about the entire time was you. How much I love you. How badly I wished it was you underneath me.

I know this doesn't make it better, but I didn't

even finish. I pretended, and then got out of there fast, and I've been in my room ever since, feeling sick because this was the room where we made love for the first time, and I've polluted everything.

I wanted you to be my only. And I've destroyed that.

But now I know that there will never be anyone for me but you. I'm not doing this ever again. I'll wait for you as long as it takes. And I won't give up until you're mine, or until you tell me that you've found someone else to love, who's worthy of you, and is a good stepdad to our daughter.

I feel sick again just writing that. But I want only what makes you happy. More than my own happiness.

And despite what I did, I loved you then, I love you still, I <u>ALWAYS</u> have and I <u>ALWAYS</u> will.

Forgive me.

Your Tim, now more than ever xxxxxxxxx

Dear Nat,

I know today was the hardest day of your life, but I had to stop and write this to let you know I am so proud of you and Eleanor. Even if I'm not going to give you this letter until we're a couple again, along with a few others I've written to you without sending over the years, I wanted to write it now while it's fresh in my mind.

I know you've been feeling alone since your mother passed, but I hope her funeral today brought you comfort, and showed you how many people care about you and will hold you up however you need while you navigate the grief.

Especially Eleanor. My heart almost burst with pride as I watched her look after you, refusing to let go of your hand the entire time. Our little sweetheart held on valiantly for that toilet break, and wouldn't go until she'd placed your hand in mine and made me promise to keep hold of it until she got back.

Thank you for keeping it there.

I've told you this a few times over the past several days, and I hope on the day you finally read this that I have conclusively proven that you can lean on me as much as you need.

You will be OK, Nat. I am so sorry you've lost both your parents at such an early stage in your life, but they raised a strong, resilient woman who is capable and intelligent. One who is already a fantastic mother, skilfully raising our little girl to be an empathetic, kind person, as she demonstrated today.

You've got this.

And if you need anything, you know I'll be there.

Loved you then

Love you still

Always have

Always will

Your Tim xxxxxxxxx

Dear Nat,

I know Sadie said something to you at her wedding today. Whatever it was, your face went pink and you looked astonished. And every time I spoke to you after that point, you couldn't meet my eye, and refused to answer when I asked what she said.

Seriously, though, what did my sister say to you to fluster you like that?! I can't sleep thinking about it...

I'd call you now, but it's 2am and I know you'd never answer anyway.

Maybe one day, when it's our time to be

together again. God, I hope you remember and can tell me.

I also hope it's not going to be much longer.

Loved you then,

Love you still,

Always have,

Always will.

Your (deeply frustrated) Tim xxxxxxxx

Natalie,

I could have lost you today.

And if I had, the regrets I would have had – about you, about us, about the time we wasted and the things we never did – would have been innumerable. And I cannot tolerate that being the case a second longer.

Enough is enough.

I love you. More than I can ever put into words. And I'm going to stop holding that back. Eleanor is old enough to cope with us being together, and the risks inherent in that; in fact, I feel certain she'd welcome it.

I'm going to make sure you focus on your recovery.

And then I'm going to take that leap of faith.

Catch me. Please.

If there's one thing the accident has proven to me, it's that there is no living without you.

I loved you then

I love you so much still

I always have

And I know I always will.

Yours forever,

Tim xxxxxxxxx

Newsletter sign-up

Want to stay informed about my latest news and upcoming releases, AND claim a free copy of Sauce, my masked man, dad bod, roommates to lovers romance novella with kink content?

Sign up to my monthly newsletter via https://lizziestanleyauthor.myflodesk.com/newsletter and claim this FREE book, exclusive to subscribers only!

Acknowledgements

As ever, it's hard to know where to begin here, but I'll give it my best shot!

Thank you to Sandra Maldo for another spectacular cover design (she also did the new covers for the Wishbone Tattoos series reboot, and they are LUSH). You have such a gift!

To Natalie and Christina, with whom awesome plans are afoot. I love you both tons.

To Aisling, Billie, and Caroline - you guys are amazing and one of my favourite parts of my days.

To all my girls in the UK Smut Authors WhatsApp chat - kisses to you all!

To my readers - you are appreciated more than you know. Special mention to Tasha, Geornesha, Michelle, Evie, Tanya, Brittany, Alyssa, Bethany, and Magi - thank you so much for your enthusiasm and kindness. Hugs and kisses for you all.

To Holly, who knows full well why. Can't wait to get our Art the Clown tattoos together. I love you more than true crime documentaries AND extreme horror movies PUT TOGETHER. I know, wow, right?

To all of my lovely friends not already mentioned -

including but not limited to Viv, Matt, Jack, Neill, Kate, Veronika, Andrew, Cat, Malcolm, Veronica, Jen, Hester, Gail... I couldn't last a day without you all.

To Karlo, despite the fact that he can't read this and wouldn't give a shit even if he could. May you have lovely rabbit chasing dreams every night and all the Bonios you could want. Thank you for your help keeping me sane in the second half of 2024.

To Mum - I miss you every single day, and I hope I can make you proud. Be at peace, and I love you to the moon and back always.

And, of course, to Mark, for everything you have done and continue to do. For seeing me through the darkest times of my life and reminding me that there is light. For loving me day in and day out, and letting me love you back. I can't even put it into sufficient words. 'Mushroom' just about covers it. PS nice arse.

ALSO BY LIZZIE STANLEY:

The Wishbone Tattoos trilogy:

What We Deserve - a hurt/comfort workplace romance

What We Need - the book that makes everyone cry (CHECK TWs)

What We Want - a best friends to lovers, black cat/golden retriever romance

Standalone:

That Perfect Fit - a short and steamy office romance novella with a truly unique hero - perfect for hitting your reading goals!

All available on Kindle Unlimited. Hyperlinks above take you to universal links.

Free book!

Sauce - a masked man, dad bod, roommates to lovers romance novella with kinky scenes - free and exclusive to my monthly newsletter subscribers only! Sign up via **https:// lizziestanleyauthor.myflodesk.com/newsletter** and claim your free copy now!

Lizzie loves to hear from her readers, so please feel free to email her via lizziestanley.author@gmail.com!

You can also follow her on Instagram and TikTok to find out more about upcoming releases...

Printed in Dunstable, United Kingdom